The Devil in
Ol' Rosie

LOUISE MOERI

The Devil in Ol' Rosie

Atheneum Books for Young Readers
NEW YORK   LONDON   TORONTO   SYDNEY   SINGAPORE

Atheneum Books for Young Readers
An imprint of Simon & Schuster Children's Publishing Division
1230 Avenue of the Americas,
New York, New York 10020

Book design by Michael Nelson
The text of this book is set Charlotte.

Printed in the United States of America.
2 4 6 8 10 9 7 5 3 1
Library of Congress Catologing-in-Publication Data
Moeri, Louise.
The devil in Ol' Rosie / by Louise Moeri.
p.   cm.
Summary: Sent into the wilderness of eastern Oregon in 1907
to round up the family's escaped horses, twelve-year-old
Wart struggles against great dangers before gaining
his father's respect.
ISBN 0-689-82614-1 (alk. paper)
[1. Fathers and sons—Fiction. 2. Frontier and pioneer life—
Fiction. 3. Horses—Fiction. 4. Ranch life—Fiction.] I. Title.
PZ7.M7214 De 2001
[Fic]—dc21   99-047053

FIRST
EDITION

Donnie & Jenene
Kaylynn
Kaitlin
Tyler

* * *

Dana & Brian
Jeraon
Michael
Mariah
Jori

one

"OL ROSIE'S LED THE HORSES OFF AGAIN!" PA'S voice was like a shaft of cold steel jabbing me under my warm quilts. "Get up, Wart. You got to go after them."

I opened my eyes. It was still black dark, and the loft was so cold, there were ice crystals on the edge of the quilts where my breath had left a little moisture. I pulled my head in like a turtle and huddled down deep in the warm feather bed.

"Get up, Wart." Pa poked me in the ribs with his hard hand. I shut my eyes quick and pretended I was still asleep. Even when you are twelve years old, sometimes that will work. For a little while.

"Wart! Roll out! *Now!*" My name is John,

but Pa calls me Wart. I guess that's the way he sees me—hard, bumpy, and not much use. But he needed me now. He grabbed the quilts and peeled them off of me. It was like falling into ice-cold springwater as the November air wrapped itself around me. My long-handle underwear didn't even slow it down.

Pa had on his long-handles, too, with just his pants pulled on over them, but he didn't even look cold. His hair wasn't combed, and three days' beard made him look even darker in the faint light coming up through the trapdoor. But there's this thing about Pa: I don't think that the cold—or heat or dark—has the guts to lay ahold of him. *I* sure wouldn't. . . .

Eyes barely opening, then, I rolled over, and my feet hit the bare wood floor. It felt like sheet ice with splinters. I stood up, with one hand windmilling around behind me. I was hoping I could grab a quilt and wrap it around me, but Pa stamped to the other end of the bunk and grabbed up my shirt and pants and boots.

"Put these on," he said. "I'm fixing you some breakfast—"

"Ma—?" I fumbled out, still barely awake.

"Ma—she's—took sick—" Pa shoved my clothes at me, and I clamped my hands over them. Ma—sick? That meant—oh. That meant—

I sat down suddenly. Well, yes, I knew it had been getting on for the time when she was to have the baby, but I guess I'd thought she'd just have it during a night, like she did with Davy, and I'd get up one morning and there it would be. I'd never thought it would have anything to do with me—or that I'd be stuck with a rotten job like going after runaway horses, just because a baby was being born. . . .

Pa jerked around and strode back to the hole in the floor of the loft and started down the ladder to the kitchen below. Now I could smell the smokey kitchen stove, the coal-oil lamp on the table. He stopped—shoulders and head still above the floor. "Hurry up," he grunted. "I'll fix you somethin' to eat. You got to get goin'—"

Yeah, Pa—I got to get goin'. How come you didn't send me out yesterday, if you're in such a hurry? I asked Ma once why Pa was always pushing us to hurry. She told me about the washtub and the looking glass: "Wart, when people like us get married and set up to make a living, people offer us either a washtub or a looking glass for a wedding present." I guess I looked dumb, because she went on to explain. "You got a choice. You can either use the washtub and take in washing and earn some money to eat with, or you can pick the looking glass and watch yourself starve to death. Your pa and I—we chose the washtub." So I guess that means I'm included in the washtub deal.

"Wart!" Pa's voice was beginning to get that hard edge in it. But even then I knew that part of the edge was because of Ma. It wasn't ever said, but Pa put Ma first. Always.

"Yeah—yeah, Pa—I'm coming!" I dressed as fast as I could, buttoning my shirt and ramming the tail into my pants, pulling on socks stiff with dried sweat and then my boots. Needed to pee—I had to get down to the kitchen fast enough to go outside to the outhouse before Pa had the food cooked, or else he'd throw it on the table and tell me to eat and I'd end up sitting there eating it with my belly about to burst. I turned to go. Oh—almost forgot—"'Mighty God, bless us in this day to come and may Your Son and our Savior be our guide—"

Sitting at the plank table beside the wood cookstove, I shoved fried potatoes and ham into my mouth while my father shoved orders into me. "You'll have to ride Gypsy. She was tied in the barn, so she's the only one didn't run off. She's slow, so you got to use your head. The other horses can all outrun her, so you got to head them off, or run them into a box. Ol' Rosie's bound to knock the fence down in the small pasture, but if you're lucky and they ain't moving too fast, you might catch up with them before she knocks the other fence down and they get out of the back pasture. If you do, try to pen them into that back corner where I got the fence partway around the spring. You got to get ropes on Pet an' Snip, though, because they'll follow Ol' Rosie if you don't. Once you get Pet an' Snip roped, Bejeesus and Damfool and Socks and the others will probably follow them. Molly an' Blaze might. Well anyway . . . some of them will follow."

"What about the colt? What about Ol' Rosie?" I knew the colt would be spooky and skittish, and that was bad enough, but rounding up Ol' Rosie was like rounding up a grizzly bear. She was just as likely to charge you as she was to go along with the herd.

"Colt will follow the mare—Pet will see to that. An' I don't care if I never see Ol' Rosie again as long as I live." Pa poured himself a tin cup of coffee and then set another cup beside my plate. "That horse's got a devil in her. She's cost me more than ten like her could ever earn."

Pa didn't ask for my opinion, but if he had, I'd have agreed with him. Pa had taken on Ol' Rosie, a huge red roan workhorse, as part payment on a loan, and we'd all been sorry ever since. Jim Cummins, the rancher who gave her to Pa instead of the fifty dollars Pa had loaned him when his wife died, had really handed Pa one of the worst problems we'd ever had—and on a dry-land ranch in eastern Oregon in the year of our Lord, 1907, that's saying a lot.

Not that Ol' Rosie wasn't strong. She must have Clydesdale or some other heavy breed of draft horse in her, because all by herself Rosie could pull a four-bottom plow or a hay wagon loaded with green timothy hay. She could pull it, that is, if she didn't kick the singletree to pieces, break the reins, and buck off half her harness while you were getting the tugs fastened. And getting her hitched up was the easy part. After that you had to be sure no rabbits sprang up under her nose and no funny noises attracted her attention—and Rosie was always swinging her hammerhead around looking for things that would attract her attention. She was powerful and deep-chested, and actually very smart (even those who had to drive her thought so), but she was crazy.

There are people who don't think horses go crazy, but those are people who don't have anything to do with horses. Either that or they've got them mixed up with those new automobiles you hear about, though so far I haven't heard of anybody getting kicked by a Ford. When you work with horses every day of your life, feed, brush, water, harness, drive, cuss, and depend on them every day, you get to know them. And some horses are crazy.

Pa said Ol' Rosie was crazy because when she foaled the first time, her owner left her out in a pasture that backed up to the foothills along the far side of the Ochocco Mountains. A grizzly bear came down out of the forest, smelled the blood and the new foal, and he stole that new little colt right away from her. I guess she put up an awful fight—there are claw scars all over her—but she lost her foal. And ever since, she's been crazy. Pa says she's got a devil in her.

I was still thinking about Ol' Rosie, and picturing that grizzly and the bloody fight she had put up for her colt, when I saw Pa suddenly jerk around. Then I heard it, too: a faint sound from the bedroom where Ma and Pa slept. It ended quickly, but I knew it had been Ma—crying. Pa dropped the skillet back onto the stove and turned and almost ran across the kitchen, through what Ma calls the parlor, and into the bedroom. I saw his face as he went by me—he looked scared. Only Ma can make him look like that. Then everything got very quiet.

I sat there at the table looking down at my tin plate and felt a chill begin to spread inside me. You don't grow up on a ranch without learning that birth is never easy. Ma was a strong woman—nearly as tall as Pa—but that didn't seem to make it any easier. I could still remember when Davy was born—I was eight years old—and even though he was born during the night, I could see that Ma was white-faced and tired for a long time afterward. Pa had worked out in the field all day and then come in and cooked, swept the floors, and hung the wash out to dry—only time I ever remember him doing that. And he finally let me use the hatchet to cut wood for kindling—he said he supposed I was old enough not to hack off any fingers, and I didn't. Came real close once, but I never told him about that.

But, finally, thinking about Ma and the baby coming, I realized that I'd better start figuring out what *I* had to do. Pa was going to have his hands full taking care of ma and keeping Davy out of trouble, and now I had my own job. I was going to get on the slowest horse we have and go out and try to find ten runaway horses and a colt in a country that is cut up into gullies and ridges and rimrocks and covered with juniper trees and pine forest, or shoulder-high sagebrush where, if you were lucky, you might get a good, clear look at a horse if he was tied up and no more than twenty feet away.

And there were a lot of square miles of this country that I would have to search. We had two pastures, both fenced, and the horses could be in either one of them. But I couldn't count much on their being in the low pasture, because if Ol' Rosie decides the grass looks better on the other side of the fence, she can just plow right through a barbwire fence as if it weren't even there. And if she did that, and then went on through the other fence around the back pasture, there was nothing to stop her from heading for the high mountains, with the only valuable things Pa has—his workhorses—at her heels. A rancher who loses his horses loses his ranch, too. I was eager to help, but I realized it wasn't just that this would be a hard job. This was the first time Pa had sent me after the whole herd when they'd run away. I sure didn't want to have to come home and tell Pa I'd let the horses get away from me. I really didn't want to do that. . . .

I gulped my coffee and shoved the last bite of fried potatoes and ham into my mouth and then grabbed up my plate and fork and carried them to the dry sink, where Ma—where somebody—would wash them. Then I stood there for a breath or two while I tried to think. What did I need to take with me? Something to eat. Blankets, in case I didn't get back before night. Ropes. And—a rifle? Suddenly I was gripped with a queasy feeling in my guts. I didn't want to go after those horses—maybe end up being out there alone in the mountains for a day or more—without a rifle. But—would Pa let me take one? He had taught me how to handle a gun and shoot, but I'd only been allowed to take one out by myself for a little while—an hour or two, never on a long ride like this, and never in rocky, brushy country. A lot can go wrong real fast when you have a gun and you don't know how to use it.

Then I heard him behind me, and I turned. "Pa—"

"Ain't you ready *yet?*" Pa came stomping into the kitchen. His face was dark, and his eyes narrow under his heavy black brows—never a good sign. Some people says Pa looks like he's part Indian, but he isn't. He's black Irish—his pa came over on the boat from Kilarney with everything he owned in a copper bucket.

Pa was carrying Davy, my four-year-old brother, wrapped in a quilt and still asleep. "You ought to be leavin' *now*."

"Yeah. Listen, Pa—"

"Here—help me git the boy settled over here on the bench—" He put Davy down on the hard wooden settle beside the cookstove, and I helped him tuck the quilt in around him. Davy has reddish hair like Ma, and he looks like her, too, or like her when she was little like him I guess. Davy was still so little—small even for a four-year-old—that his hand holding the quilt didn't look much bigger than a baby's. But all at once it came to me: From now on, Davy wouldn't be "the baby" any-more. And even though he makes me so mad because he tags after me and steps on Ma's garden stuff and makes noise and leaves gates open—*gates open?*

All at once I looked up at Pa. "Davy—did he leave the corral gate open? Is that how the horses got out?"

Pa stood up and, as he did, he reached

for a pair of saddlebags that were hanging on the wall. He grunted. "I reckon he did. But *you* should have watched him. *You* should have caught it."

My shoulders sagged. My fault again. Jeez—it's bad enough to be blamed for my own mistakes without Davy's thrown in, too. It would have taken my whole day just to follow Davy to keep him out of trouble. But I knew better than to argue. Pa isn't a man you argue with much. And if he was already blaming me for the horses getting out, there was no sense in even asking about the rifle now.

I went over to the row of coats hanging on nails by the door and took down my warmest fleece-lined sheepskin coat. It was a hand-me-down from Pa, and pretty big, but I would need it to ride God knows how many miles in this weather. I'd be lucky if it didn't snow. The ground was still bare, but we'd had several freezes already, and it couldn't be too long before the first heavy snow fell. The cows and horses had furred out in their heavy, hairy winter coats—too bad God didn't make people like the animals. I'd once asked Ma why He didn't do that, and she'd cut back a faint little smile. "He knew what you'd look like in fur," she'd said.

Over by the stove, Pa was wrapping biscuits in a towel. "I'm puttin' in all the bread we got, an' some cold fried ham. There's two canteens an' you'll have to take both of them. Horses can drink at the springs, but you got to be careful an' drink only clean water—"

I wound a muffler around my neck and, as I took my old black hat—also a hand-me-down from Pa—and my leather gloves off the bench by the door, I happened to look over at the wooden shelves beside the bench. On the shelves were rows of glass jars, pale green, filled with peaches. Ma had canned them last August. I'd peeled them, listening to Ma as she'd sung kind of to herself, songs like "Bringing in the Sheaves" and "When the Roll Is Called Up Yonder I'll Be There," and then she'd filled the jars and fastened on the lids and boiled them in a huge old copper tub. She'd always let me eat the little pieces that didn't fit in the last jar, so they wouldn't be wasted, she said. And even now, just thinking about those peaches, the taste, the smell, the color, made my mouth water. A jar of Ma's peaches could make even this ride better. "Can I take a jar of Ma's peaches?"

"Hell, boy, how you gonna open a jar of peaches out in the brush? Now, git out there an' saddle Gypsy. I'll bring your gear out in a minute—"

Well, no peaches. There was nothing more to say. I turned and went out into the icy darkness.

two

As I shut the door behind me I heard a scuffle off to the left, and a black and gray blur came bouncing up. I reached out and felt a pointy nose nuzzle my hand. "Yah, Trixie," I said as our little shepherd dog began to dance around me. She'd come out of her warm hole under the porch to follow me out to the barn, and she seemed tickled pink to see me. But Trixie took everything that way. She was full of prunes and ready to go anytime. In fact, the one thing Trixie didn't know how to do was back off. I've seen her hang on to a cow's tail when the cow was kicking her at every step. Trixie's a good cow dog or sheepdog. I've even seen her try to round up the chickens when they got out of the pen. If I had been going after cattle today, Trixie could have gone with me and helped me. But I was going after horses, and horses won't herd for a dog. Horses won't even herd for a rider, unless you've got a lot of riders. That's why this job today was going to be so hard. I couldn't just round up the ten horses and expect them to drift along ahead of me back to the barn like cows would. I knew I had to get them corralled—or make them think they were corralled—somewhere, get ropes on Pet and Snip, and then lead them back.

Because there *is* one thing about horses: They always have a "leader"—usually an older mare—and most of the time they will follow that leader. Most of the time. Pet, Pa's oldest mare, was the leader among our horses. There was a good chance that the other horses, Bejeesus and Damfool, Prince and Dandy and the others, would follow Pet home, and an even better chance if I could rope both Pet and Snip, because Snip always worked next to Pet (she was Pet's colt, in fact) and was like her shadow. With hard work and a lot of luck I might be able to get most of the horses back into either of the lower pastures close to home, or even—God willing and the creeks don't rise—into the home corral. A lot depended on the horses themselves, but then anytime you do something with horses, it's a toss-up as to whether they're going to do it your way or theirs. Horses are . . . well, they're like people. Pa had taught me to harness, groom, and feed, right along with teaching me never to walk behind Bejeesus and never to come up on Socks on the right side. Bejeesus will kick anything behind him he can reach; I've seen people do about the same. And Socks is blind in his right eye—you can't blame him for not wanting things to happen on his blind side.

"No," I said now as I stopped to pet Trixie and ruffle her fluffy-dog-smelling fur, "you can't go. You're no help with horses. You got to stay here."

I turned my collar up to keep the cold air out as I crossed the barn lot and lifted the heavy wooden bar on the barn door, opened it, and went in. The barn was pitch-dark, but I knew where to find Gypsy: in her stall halfway down the aisle. She was tied to her manger—which was why she hadn't run off with the other horses—and had a nice pile of manure ready for me to step into as I fumbled around in the dark. I grunted as I kicked it off my boots. I thought about brushing her down but decided against it. I crossed the barn aisle behind the horse and felt along the pegs on the wall. I chose the smaller, lighter saddle but I picked, by feeling it, the largest saddle blanket we had. It would protect Gypsy better from the scratchy brush and the cold as well as saddle sores. It put the blanket on her and went back for the saddle. When I got over with the saddle, holding it braced on my right shoulder like Pa had taught me, I started to throw it up—and realized she'd shrugged the blanket off—Went back and hung up the saddle, picked up the blanket, and put it on her again. Got the saddle and staggered across the aisle to the horse—blanket on the ground again. I was beginning to sweat. Nothing warms you up on a cold morning like saddling a horse. I let the saddle fall to the ground at my feet, grabbed the blanket out from between Gypsy's feet, and slapped it on her back. Then I hoisted the saddle—from ground level—up to my shoulder again, and with one last furious push I threw it up, and it settled into place on the blanket. As I stood there panting, the barn door crashed open. "Hellfire, Wart—ain't you got that horse saddled yet?" yelled Pa. "I got your gear out here—git a move on!"

Sure, Pa. Right away, Pa.

I reached under Gypsy's fat belly, caught the cinch, and quickly threaded the latigo through the ring. Turned and pressed my back against the horse's side to lever up high enough to tighten the cinch. Felt the mare suck in a deep breath. I whirled around, raised my foot, and kicked her sharply in the belly. Gypsy let out her breath in a rattly snort and, before she could suck in another, I yanked the cinch tight. If there's anything makes Pa mad, it's a sloppy job of saddling up. I reached up and grabbed the saddle horn and yanked it back and forth. Saddle seemed tight. Then I grabbed a bridle and put it on her, fighting the bit in between her big, hard teeth. I left the halter on under the bridle because there was always a chance on a long ride like this that I'd have to get off and tie the horse up, and you need a halter to do that. Then I took two lengths of rope from nails on the wall and fastened them to the saddle horn. I'd need them to lead Pet and Snip home. When it was all done, I caught the reins and, pulling like on a dead weight—Gypsy wasn't dumb enough to think it was going to be nice to go outside on a morning like this—I backed her out of the stall and staggered out the barn door with her stumbling along behind me.

Outside, Pa was standing there with a pile of stuff on the ground. Trixie was there, too, bouncing around Pa's feet. She probably still thought she would get to go with me.

"I'm ready," I said. Looking around at the barn lot, barely able to see fences and sheds and watering troughs in the gray cold light, I hoped God didn't strike me dead for lying. I sure wasn't ready, but I was going anyhow.

Pa reached up and fastened the two canteens, linked together, on the left front of the saddle. Then he tied on a roll of blankets and threw the saddlebags over the saddle behind the blankets and tied all the strings. I noticed he handled the saddlebags kind of gently, but I didn't ask why. Pa gets cranky when you ask too many questions. He's not like Ma—she'll make a guessing game out of it, or tell a joke. Pa just lets you know that you ought to have known the answer before you asked.

Then Pa reached up and grabbed the saddle horn and shook it. The saddle slid around like it was on grease. Oh, hell. The cinch was hanging two inches below Gypsy's belly. "Pa—I tightened the cinch! I *did*—"

Grimly, Pa punched Gypsy's gut again

and yanked the latigo into tight turns that would hold that saddle on if I rode Gypsy off a cliff. "You got to go back an' check. Always check yourself, boy. You can't take chances on nothin'."

"Pa," I said, and I have no idea why I said it, "horses are just no damn good. Some people are getting rid of them. I read in a newspaper about people who are making machines. Tractors, they call them. An' they don't . . . run off."

Pa turned to look at me. "Massey-Harris," he said, "an' International Harvester. An' they cost more than this whole damn ranch is worth. Even if they don't run off."

"If I was rich," I muttered, hunched against the cold and dreading the day that was coming, "if I was rich, I'd buy a tractor to farm with."

Pa gave me a long, hard look. "Wart," he said at last, "if you was rich, you wouldn't *be* a farmer. Now, git on—"

I threw Gypsy's reins over her neck and gathered them in my left hand, put my left foot in the stirrup, and swung up into the saddle. It was like coming down

astride of a block of ice. "An' there's automobiles, too," I said, half-choked. "They
don't take horses. They just go by themselves."

Pa slanted a hard look up at me.
"That's just what you're doin' now, Wart—
goin' by yourself." I stared down. Was *Pa*
joking?

Then Pa reached up and fastened
something to the right front of my saddle. I
looked down at it and stopped breathing.

It was a rifle scabbard.

My heart started to pound, but I didn't
say a word as he slid his old .22 rifle into
the scabbard and handed me a box of shells.
My hand hardly shook at all as I slid the
box into my inside pocket. It felt . . . good.
Square, heavy, *good*.

"Wart." Pa reached up and laid his
hand on Gypsy's neck, and looking down I
could just see the outlines of his face, his
back and shoulders hunched inside his
old coat. And even though he was below
me, just for a second I felt him speak to
me as if we were on some kind of level.
"I'm layin' a hard job on you. But—it's all I

can do. We got to have the horses. I got to stay here with Ma. I'm—depending on you." Then he stepped back. "You better git goin'. And—be careful—"

That was all. I reined Gypsy around and kicked her into a trot, heading her out the corral gate that Pa held open for me. Gypsy leaned into her reins as I pointed her nose up the slope behind the house. I turned to look back once. Pa had turned away toward the house without so much as a second look. I knew he would carry water, keep the fires up, watch Davy— I knew he would stand by Ma.

And I knew something else: I knew I could not come back without the horses.

three

OUTSIDE THE GATE I LOOKED UP AND OUT OVER the long slope of ridge that dropped down from the high hogback to the south, to slant gradually northward to where the barbwire fence cut it off from the big rye field. This was what we called the "small pasture." I would make a circle around it. If the horses weren't there, then I would have to go on much farther and make a circle out of the big pasture. This small pasture was the regular horse pasture—fairly clear of brush and trees, and with plenty of bunchgrass but no water. That made it easier to bring the horses into the barn when they were needed, because they got thirsty by the end of a day feeding on dry grass.

I've brought the horses in lots of times from the small pasture; hard as it is to run horses, it's not too bad here because they'll make for the water. Of course, one and then another will try to bolt, but you keep heading them off and, finally, as you come down the long slope to the open corral gate, they start to run, tails streaming and heads stretched out. And they are beautiful, then—even potbellied old work-horses with swaybacks and hammer-heads.

I guess God figured His horses looked pretty running, and that's why He made them loose-triggered, quick to run at any excuse, or none at all. I just wish He'd have made them a little less quick to kick and bite and balk and step on your feet, but I don't mention this, especially around Ma. Ma says God made everything, and made it the way He wanted it. Makes you wonder sometimes why He made some of the stuff. Now, I like rain in summer, but why did He make dust storms? And grass is good, but Russian thistle is mean. Wheat and rye are good—but did we really need fireweed? And why do people get broken legs, and cattle die of anthrax?

Of course, there's yellowbells to pick in the spring, and new grass, and fiddle music and jokes and hot stew and biscuits on a cold day. . . . Maybe it all evens out— if you could ever see it all. . . .

But I couldn't see it all right now. All I could see was the pasture I was in and the one that lies on the other side of the fence. The big pasture runs the full east-west length of the ranch and beyond, and lies south of this one. There is no gate between the two, but there had been times when we'd had to do this before, and there is a place in the fence toward the far corner where Pa had cut the wires and made some extra turns with them around two of the fence posts, and you could unwind them and lead a horse through. And if I found that Ol' Rosie had knocked the fence down anywhere along it before I got to that place, I would have to take enough time to put it all back together before going on. I knew Pa would have slipped a hammer and some fencing staples into my saddlebags. There's two things Pa gets mad about: gates left open and somebody seeing that a fence needs fixing and they don't do it. Pa says they save the hottest places in hell for people who don't take care of their fences. . . .

But once I got beyond the first fence, I would be in the big pasture, and there the job of hunting the horses would get much harder. The small pasture is maybe a couple of square miles in area but fairly open. One good turn around it halfway up the ridge and I could be sure the horses weren't there.

But the big pasture is a different world. Pa's ranch includes this high, rough stretch of ridges and gullies. He had fenced it in, but he never uses it except as summer range for beef cattle. The lower stretch of the pasture nearest the ranch house is bad enough, but from there it slopes up steeply into the high, main hogback ridge scattered with sage and juniper that give way to heavy pine forest at the top. It hadn't been part of Grandpa's original homestead, but Grandpa had bought it up, one piece at a time, from other ranchers who went broke or just got disgusted with having to work like dogs the year around and sold out and went off to look for easier ways to make a living, maybe in The Dalles or in Portland. They left, but Grandpa stayed, and after him my Pa. And he still has the big pasture, and even though it's a dog's job to round up cattle there, he has made money off of it. Every summer Pa would turn whatever half-grown steers we had up there, and they would be fat and sleek when we brought them down to sell off in October. Three weeks ago, just after our school shut down because the teacher left because she got consumption, Pa and I had rounded up the yearlings—and it was real fresh in my memory how I hated the cut-up and overgrown nightmare that is called the "big pasture." Even the fence that runs around it is a bad dream. It isn't a real fence running in a straight line with good, solid, hewn-to-size posts set in the ground. It's made of mile after mile of barbwire strung from tree to tree so that it zigzags like something built by two drunks and a blind man. And although the fence does hold the yearlings in from wandering off, it does nothing at all to keep out whatever bear, deer, cougar, bobcat, and lynx still live and hunt among the high ridges. And Pa had told me, the day we brought the cattle down, that back just a few years ago, when there were still Cayuse Indians living free in these mountains, they could move around half a mile from our house and you couldn't see them. Today I would be looking for a small band of black and brown horses in country where a party of thirty Indians in war paint, mounted on splashy-colored pintos and Appaloosas, would have been hard to see.

As we neared the crest of the low ridge, I halted Gypsy and turned to look back. The ranch house sits like a blanket Indian, low against the earth, with windows only half-lit by coal-oil lamps. The roofline is broken by two chimneys—one made of stone from the fireplace in Ma's parlor, and the other made of tin stovepipe that comes up from the cookstove in the kitchen. Faint trails of smoke rose from both of them. Pa must have been trying to keep the house warm so that Ma would feel better. And of course when the new baby came, it couldn't stand the cold like the rest of us.

For a minute I thought about the new baby. Would it be another boy, like Davy, or a girl? Neither Pa nor Ma ever talked about the baby, like no one was supposed to notice how Ma had changed and the way her dresses were way out in front, and how she walks now, slow and awkward and bending backward to balance herself. But they both said and did things that meant "baby" even so. A couple of weeks ago Pa had gone up to the loft where I sleep and brought down Davy's old cradle and took it out to his shop and replaced a couple of spindles in the sides. He took a wood rasp and smoothed the rockers, and even repainted the row of hearts and roses across the head and foot. Pa has a good hand for drawing and painting, and he can make real nice things out of wood. He had made the cradle to begin with for me, and then fixed it up again for Davy when he came.

I always like to hang around Pa when he's working with wood. He hardly ever gets mad then—his face looks kind of absentminded, like he's laid his grouchiness down somewhere and forgotten to pick it up again. But his hands—they seem to know exactly what to do with the saw, the hammer, the rasp, the carving knife, and chisel. He doesn't seem to tell them—they just know. I wish—God, I wish my hands knew all the things Pa's hands know. . . .

While Pa was fixing the cradle, Ma had called me from stacking firewood, and had sent me up to the loft to bring down a box for her.

Ma hadn't said so much as a word to me about the baby, of course, or how it happened that she was going to have it—though I knew about all that—but she'd told me to bring her the box of old baby clothes that was sitting at the end of my bunk. And when she'd taken the clothes out and washed them, I'd had to hang them on ropes strung up across the kitchen. It sure was hard to believe that Davy or I was ever small enough to wear those things. I almost asked her once if these things could fit on a real baby, but I didn't. People don't talk about things like that. But I did measure the size of one thing called a "wrapper"—and it wasn't as wide at the shoulders as my hand with the fingers only half-opened. How could a thing be that small and still live?

Now as I looked beyond the house, down the slope to where the barn is, I didn't see any flash of lantern light that would mean Pa was getting ready to milk. I knew he would have to take care of Ma first and let the cows wait, as well as the hogs and chickens. If we lived in a town, like Prineville, maybe, or at least a lot closer to it, Ma could have had a doctor help her, or at least some other women. But we were so far from even the nearest ranch—and that was the Jorgensen place, and there weren't any women there—that Pa couldn't even have gone to fetch help and got back in time.

If it hadn't been for Ol' Rosie leading

off the horses, I could at least have been there to take care of the chores for Pa while he took care of Ma. I can't milk as fast as Pa, but I can milk enough to get by, especially now since most of the cows are dry. And I can fork down hay and carry the slop bucket from the kitchen out to the pigs, and throw out cracked wheat for the chickens and hunt out the few eggs they're laying now in cold weather. But of course now I couldn't do any of that because of Ol' Rosie and the devil in her that made her crazy, the devil that could even cost Pa the ranch, if we really lost the horses.

And all at once as I sat there on Gypsy, looking down the slope of the hill at the ranch, it seemed to me that the barbwire fence that circles the house and Ma's garden and the barns and corrals and sheds was like a stockade fence around some old forgotten frontier fort. And Ma and Pa and Davy and me were all that was left to keep it going, to keep the sagebrush and junipers and tumbleweeds from taking it back. The ranch is back up so close to the Wallowa Mountains that the deer and elk come down in winter to pick off bits of hay left in the fields, and more than once a bear or cougar has killed a calf. Wildness is just waiting to take over.

It wouldn't take much for this fort to fall. . . .

It took me probably a little over two hours to do a careful job of searching the small pasture. I hadn't expected to find the horses there, so I wasn't disappointed when I didn't turn up any. Ol' Rosie took off like this about once a year, and when she lit out, she didn't stop till she ran herself into a box canyon or a ridge even she couldn't climb. But with Pa and me working together, they could be rounded up and brought back. Alone, a single rider was going to have a hard time of it.

As I circled the small pasture I had tried to watch the ground for tracks. This late in the year the bunchgrass is pretty well eaten down, and the sage is scattered. I'm not as good at tracking as Pa, so I couldn't pick out the freshest tracks, made last night, from those a day or so older. Anyway, the horses were turned out here at least once a week on Sundays, so there would always be tracks crisscrossing these open slopes. The place to try to pick up tracks would be in the big pasture, and the place to start looking for them was wherever I found the fence knocked down.

As it turned out, I didn't have to go all the way to where Pa had fixed the fence so we could get through. The sun was well up, and I was just beginning to feel a little warmth from it on my back when right ahead I saw a fence post lying flat on the ground. It was about a quarter of a mile from the place where Pa had made the pass-through, and in a place where the ground is so covered with rocks that posts, instead of being sunk in postholes, are braced up with big piles of rocks.

"Oh . . . no." I pulled Gypsy to a stop and sat there looking at the mess. Ol' Rosie had knocked down not one—not two—but three fence posts. The wires lay on the ground, scraping over the rocks, and the middle post was snapped in two.

And I had to fix this mess before I could go on. Otherwise, the horses could swing around behind me and keep going back and forth through the downed fence, and I would spend the rest of my life out here trying to catch up with them.

I climbed down off Gypsy, and she heaved a big sigh and dangled her head down like she was worn out. She coughed a couple of times and ran her tongue out over her bit. Gypsy always tried to make you think she could hardly make it another step, much less another mile. That's another one of those things about horses—a horse can be staggering and limping along like he's half-dead, but you turn his head for home and he'll take off like a racehorse. I knew Gypsy wasn't really tired. Not yet . . .

I peeled my gloves off, stuck them under the saddle horn, and stood there for a minute looking at the busted fence. I had to pick out the best place to lead Gypsy across it, because when I put it all back together again, she and I would have to be on the far side. The barbwires were down, all right, but there was only one place where they were actually on the ground. Or on the rocks—because mostly they lay across a huge, flat slab of the blackish rocks that are dotted all over this country. Pa says they're old lava rocks. I say they're hard and ugly. And Gypsy said, when I gathered her reins and tried to lead her onto the slab so she could cross the downed fence, that they were slick under her hooves and she wasn't going to walk on them.

I pulled on the reins.

Gypsy stood like a horse made of iron.

I pulled forward.

She pulled back.

I clenched my teeth and threw my weight against the reins.

Gypsy swung her head—with me dangling on the reins—and looked off out over the flat land to the north and watched a hawk circling up in the sky.

I dug in my heels and pulled some more. Nothing. Finally I raised my foot and kicked her in the belly.

Gypsy let out a snort and lunged forward onto the slab. I leaped after her, lost one rein, kept the other, tried to guide her over the wires—and almost made it. The last wire snaked up and then jabbed down, biting into her leg just above her left hind hoof.

Gypsy squealed and plunged forward, forcing the barbs on the wire deeper into her leg. I clamped my hand on the only rein I still had and reached out bare-handed to pull the wire away from her foot. I felt the barbs rip across my palm. Blood spurted out between my fingers.

In a second I had the wire down and off her foot. Gypsy was snorting and danc-ing and holding up her cut foot. She was trembling, and her eyes were wide open and rolling—she was bleeding a little, and a horse goes crazy when it smells blood. Any blood, even her own. Especially her own.

I was shaking, too, as I led her away from the fence. I stopped close to a little cluster of small juniper trees. Gypsy leaned her head down and snorted up a big puff of dust. She was still holding her cut foot up, and I knew it hurt her.

For a second or two I stood there. I was

so mad, I could cuss. First real obstacle, and I had messed up. Not only did I let my horse get cut up, but I cut myself up, too. And out here there is no hot water to wash with or use for a saltwater soak, no clean bandages, no Watkins Salve to put on the wounds to help keep them from getting infected. And a person can die from infection. I've seen Ma turn white as a sheet when Pa cut his hand with the ax, or Davy fell out of a tree and ran big splinters into his fingers. Ma always reminds me that President Lincoln's son died from a blistered heel that got infected.

Pa just reminds me that I ought to be smart enough to stay in one piece.

four

BEFORE I STARTED WORK ON THE FENCE I TOOK the rifle out of the scabbard and carried it over to a safe place where I could reach it fast if a rattlensake happened to turn up— though that is not very likely in November. I was careful not to pick a place where there was loose dirt and the rifle could fall. If there was one thing I was going to do right on this ride, it was take care of that rifle. I knew Pa had gone way out on a limb to let me bring it, and I wasn't about to let him down by shooting myself in the foot. Then I went back and unsaddled Gypsy and tethered her inside a clump of junipers where there was a nice patch of bunchgrass for her to eat and she would be out of the wind.

• • •

It took me close to three hours, I guess, to put the fence back up. I didn't have a watch, but I could tell that the sun was about as high in the sky as it would get today when I heaved the last rock up and staggered over to throw it onto the pile holding the middle post. I had found a dead juniper nearby and broken two pieces off it to nail like splints onto the broken post, and then I propped all three posts back up and started piling rocks around them to make them stand. I finished it off by stapling the wires back onto the posts. It was slow, hard, dirty work, and I was ready to drop when I had it all up and reasonably steady.

I was just picking up a couple of nails I had dropped, when I noticed a small, smooth piece of wood lying beside the last post. It was about six inches long and maybe an inch and a half wide, and came to rough, ragged points on both ends. I picked it up. I could take that home, I thought. I could whittle it into a little toy boat for Davy. Davy doesn't have hardly any toys to play with. There's one rubber ball, but whenever he throws it, Trixie runs and grabs it and then she goes off to chew on it, and he can't find it for a week. And he's got three or four little horses and cows that Pa carved for him, and a hoop to roll, and in summer Ma always fixes him a swing on the poplar tree by the house, but it's not enough to keep him busy. He pesters me to play games with him. So once last summer I told him we'd play hide-and-seek, and for him to go and hide—and then I forgot to go look for him. He went to sleep hidden in the woodshed, and Ma nearly went crazy before we found him. I felt kind of sorry for Davy and Ma, too, but then Pa thrashed me for "losing" him, so I quit feeling sorry for them and felt sorry for myself.

But that was last summer. And it really wasn't Davy's fault I got whipped. . . .

I slipped the little piece of wood into the deep pocket of my coat. I'll make him a boat, I thought, and give it to him for Christmas. And already I could almost tell how that wood would feel when I got my hands on a knife and started to whittle on it. Maybe Pa and I are a little bit alike, that way.

With the fence finished, I got the saddle-bags from the saddle and found the warmest place to sit among the trees. I was so hungry, I was shaking but I made myself sit still long enough to say the blessing Ma had hammered into me: "For what we are about to receive, dear Lord, we thank Thee—"

I unfastened the small buckle that held the flap down on one side of the saddle-bags and looked in. There were two or three packages wrapped in towels and tied with string, and I only opened the first two I found. Biscuits in one bundle and some pieces of fried ham in the other. I grabbed a biscuit and a piece of ham and started biting off big chunks.

I'd never tasted anything so good. Even with no butter, no jam, that biscuit was the best bread I ever ate. And the ham, greasy and cold, was salty and rich and full of flavor. I stopped once for a drink of water from the small canteen. The sun in the little clump of trees was warm, and I had fixed the fence and now I was eating, and I felt a lot better.

I did have the sense to trickle a little water over the barbwire cuts on my hand. They were ragged and ugly, but I cleaned them as well as I could. I had nothing to bandage them with, so all I could do was wash them. I also got up and went over to Gypsy and ran some of the water through her cuts. She snorted and raised her foot to kick me, but I jumped back in time. None of the cuts—mine or hers—was deep, but any cut is a cut, and I knew I had made my first mistake for the day. Pa would have quite a bit to say to me when he saw what had happened.

And all at once, standing there with my hand on Gypsy's neck, I began to feel alone. God-awful alone. The juniper trees were like people who speak a different language. To each other. The rocks didn't even do that. And Pa wasn't here to yell at me and keep me from making mistakes. Ma wasn't here to tell me, "Don't eat so fast. There'll be some left for the next meal—"

The next meal? Suddenly I stopped thinking about being alone and started thinking about being hungry. The next meal I would get to eat—maybe even the next two or three meals—would be out of the saddlebags. And those bags aren't very big. How much food was left?

I went over to the saddlebags and opened the flaps. I had eaten three biscuits and most of one slice of the ham. That left eight biscuits and a little more than two full slices of ham. All at once I realized it didn't look like much. Very carefully I gathered the biscuits together and wrapped them up tight in the towel. I wrapped the ham up and then fitted the two bundles back into the saddlebag. The bag still looked fairly full, but I was afraid that was because the towels took up a lot of room.

Slowly I got to my feet. I stood there for a few heartbeats, thinking. It was past noon, more likely an hour or more past noon, and all I had found so far was the place where the horses had gotten out. I had fixed the fence as well as I could, and now I had to go on to the hardest part of the search. And in this big pasture it could easily take till sundown to find the horses.

For one thing, I would have to stop and let Gypsy rest every so often. I had to make the best use of everything I had to find the horses, get ropes on Pet and Snip, and head for home. There was no time to waste thinking about being lonely, or anything else. If I didn't find the horses before dark—

But I decided not to think about that. Yet.

The first thing to do was saddle up, and the second was to make several circles around the break in the fence and pick up the horses' tracks in the big pasture.

Gypsy unloaded her blanket twice and managed to bite my finger when I bridled her. She tried to step on my foot, but her hoof came down on a small rock, so I hardly got pinched at all. "Just you wait," I said as her tail swished across my face, "Them tractors will get cheaper all the time. An' you haven't even heard about automobiles yet—" I had to kick her belly twice to get the cinch tight but when I finally tested it, the saddle felt like it was nailed to her back. Then I tied the saddlebags on good. I put the rifle into the scabbard last and made sure the shells were still in my pocket. At last I swung up into the saddle, but then I remembered Pa telling me to "check myself," so I made a thorough search along the fence and around the clearing to make sure I hadn't left the hammer or something behind. Nothing. It was a good job.

Finally I turned Gypsy's nose to the right and began to make a series of widening circles on either side of the break in the fence. Sooner or later I would cut across the horses' tracks.

And I did. They were hard to pick out, but one good thing about Ol' Rosie was that she's heavier than the other horses, and her hooves were so big that she made a strong, clear print. In fact, that may have been the only good thing about her.

I found them on the third circle. The trail was not easy to pick out because Ol' Rosie's tracks—she was in the lead, of course—were blurred by the others as they followed her, but I was satisfied that these tracks were fresh. And they headed straight up the flank of the high ridge toward the trees.

five

To begin with I thought the best thing to do was follow the tracks. And at first, when all the horses were banded close together, it was at least clear what direction they were going. But then, maybe a hundred yards beyond the downed fence and well up onto the ridge, I realized that the horses had spread out. That was a natural thing for them to do. When they are moving fast, running away, they stay close together, but when they know they are outside the regular pasture and free, or think they are, they fan out and start to feed. The one thing a horse has to do is eat, because it takes an awful lot of food to keep him going. I could count on them moving much slower now, and a lot of the time they'd have their heads down grazing. I might even get a chance to come up fairly close to them before they saw me, if I could just make good enough time now. Even so, I knew the only chance I had to bring them in was to be able to run them into some kind of a corner and get ropes on Pet and Snip. Fast. *Very* fast.

It was about the middle of the after-noon—I could tell from the slant of the sun-light—when I came up even with the first deep ravine that funnels down off the high ridge. And here was where I had to change directions. From where I was I couldn't see down into the ravine, especially since the bottom of it is extra brushy and the junipers there are very full and wide. Ravines catch runoff water, so that's where trees grow best, and of course that's where the best grass is, too. Besides, I could see that some or maybe all of the horses had drifted down toward the ravine. They knew where the best grass was, as well as I did.

So I turned Gypsy down the side of the ridge toward the ravine-bottom. I knew I would have to get off the horse and search it on foot because climbing the rocky cut would be hard for Gypsy, and only wear her out faster. If the horses were in the ravine, there was a good chance that I could quickly haul some dead brush or a fallen log across it, making them think for a minute they were penned in, and if I was lucky I might get the ropes on Pet and Snip and be ready to head for home. If I was lucky. Of course, they could hear me and spook and come charging down and run right over me on their way out. I've heard Pa tell stories of men who let themselves get into a place like that, where a bunch of horses or cattle stampeded over them. Most of those guys spend the rest of their lives walking with a limp, if they can walk at all. I had to look for the horses in the ravines—but I'd have to keep my eyes and ears open for the slightest noise or movement.

At the place where the ravine closed in to about ten feet across, I stopped Gypsy and got off. I tied her halter rope to the trunk of a juniper where she would be right close to the bank. Then I took the two lead ropes off the saddle and started up the ravine. I could see that the horses had come up this way, feeding on the grass that is tall and rank here even this late in the fall. They had left some manure, and their tracks were there, though blurred.

I climbed the rocky trench for maybe ten minutes, keeping very quiet, but before long I began to feel that the horses were not here, although tracks showed in the soft, sandy places that they had been. For one thing, I couldn't hear them. Horses can be quiet, but not absolutely silent, and I couldn't hear a thing. No stomping hooves, no swishing tails, no grunting coughs, no long, dusty sneezes.

And as I rounded the last outcrop of rocks and came up against the bare stone wall that lines the highest end of the ravine—where in spring a little waterfall would pour snow-melt down off the ridge—I saw that the small, open place was empty. The horses had been here, all right, but they had turned back down the ravine and escaped from this tight little pocket before I could get there.

But then I also saw something else.

Against the smooth side of a pale gray upright slab of rock at the back of the ravine was a ragged red smear. Blood.

I stood there and felt my own blood getting colder than the air in that sunless, rocky slit. Blood. Blood means a wound, and a wound means that one of the horses had been attacked. This wasn't a smear left by something like the wire cuts I had, or like Gypsy had on her hind leg. The smear on the rock was at least twelve inches long, maybe a couple of inches wide. It took a lot of blood to make a mark like that. And it was three feet up the side of the rock: That meant that one of the horses had been wounded—*how?*—along the shoulder, the ribs, or the rump.

It also meant that now I had two more things to watch out for: One was the horses themselves. because if one of them was hurt, they would all be wild and spooky and on the prod, even worse than usual, ready to bite, kick, or strike out at anything or anyone they saw as a threat. And, right from that moment, the other thing to fear was . . . whatever had attacked the horse. And I had left the rifle in the scabbard on the saddle.

I turned and flung myself back down the ravine, running and jumping from rock to rock. I managed not to drop the two lead ropes, but only because my fingers had frozen around them. I stumbled and half-fell and finally slid to a halt just a few feet from Gypsy.

I was still shaking as I got to my feet and walked over to her. As I tied the ropes back to the saddle horn and tightened the cinch, I wondered what Pa would have said if he had seen me climb into a boxed-in ravine without a rifle and where, if the horses had been there, they could have killed me.

"Check yourself," Pa had said. "Always check yourself."

It took me probably half an hour to work my way back up the far side of the ravine and beyond, following the blurry trail of hoofprints. The sun was well past halfway down to the western horizon, and when I turned to look at it, to try to figure out how much more daylight I still had, I could see that a bank of heavy gray clouds was rolling in from the west. That's great, I thought. It isn't bad enough I'm out here in the brush chasing a band of horses and one of them is hurt and now it's getting on for dark—But if those clouds keep coming, there'll be snow flying before I can make it home. And if it happens to be a bad storm—well, people have gotten lost and frozen to death in a snowstorm when they were within a half mile of home.

I kicked Gypsy with my boot heels and slapped her on the rump with the end of one of the ropes, to try to get her to move faster, but it was no use, and I knew it. Gypsy was a slow, sleepy pony at least seventeen years old, and she wasn't much good for anything but bringing in the milk cows or carrying food and water to Pa when he was plowing or haying all day. The little mare had gone about as far as she had it in her to go today, and she certainly wasn't going to go any faster than she was going now.

It wasn't that I was so far from the house in miles—by now I was probably only three miles from the gate into the home corral, though I'd covered a lot more in a big circle to get here—but it would be dusk by four-thirty and full flat dark by five or five-thirty, and from here on the way would be up and down steep slopes and fighting trees, brush and rocks all the way. I might as well face it: The cold, hard truth was that there was no way I could make it back tonight, even if I found the horses in the next hour.

I pulled Gypsy to a halt and sat there in the saddle for a few minutes. I let her "blow"—she was panting heavily from the sharp climb already—and I had to do some hard thinking.

By now I was about a quarter of a mile below the crest of the ridge and starting down the rounded flank of the next ravine, with one ravine—the one where I had seen the blood smeared on the rock—behind me, and three more ahead. I might be able to search the next deep, brush-filled gulley before dark but—what then?

And I *knew* what, even though I hated to think about it. I had to find someplace to make a camp for the night. And it would have to be in one of the ravines. I had to balance the threat of whatever had attacked the horses, which could back me into a corner in the ravine, against the much more certain fact that Gypsy and I would both nearly freeze trying to camp overnight up here on the exposed, windy ridge. And as I looked back once more, I could see the clouds moving fast, eating up the fading light. I had to find a safe place to camp. Now.

"Damn," I said. "Damn." And I turned Gypsy's head downhill toward the bottom of the ravine.

It was cold and silent and almost dark in the ravine as Gypsy slid down the last drop to the water-scoured floor. It was too dark for me now to see any tracks, even in the sandy places, and there was no sense in pretending I was still looking for the horses. Wherever they were now, I had run out of time and daylight, and the search was off till morning. What I needed right now was grass for Gypsy and water, and a sheltered place to keep off some of the cold where I could build a fire and lay my bedroll for the night. I had never in my life had to do something like this, but I've heard Pa and Grandpa tell stories about being caught out at night or in a storm. I knew what I had to do.

I swung down off Gypsy and felt my legs wobble and twitch when my feet hit the ground. I was stiff from the cold, and the insides of my knees were beginning to ache from the pressure of holding on to the horse. I stamped my feet and bent my legs to loosen the cramps and get the blood circulating faster. Then Gypsy jerked sharply on the reins and leaned away from me toward a shadowy patch of grass at the bottom of the bank. She was hungry. Worse than that, she was probably very thirsty. She would have to have water, and soon. I had to see that she got both feed and water first, and then I could think about myself, and the awful empty feeling in my own belly.

I knew there were at least two springs in this big stretch of ridges and rocks, and also some other places almost as good where the rocky ravines form deep pools that hold rainwater for a long time. We'd had a heavy rain about a week ago, and if my memory was working right now, this ravine had one of those pools about a foot deep at the upper end. Since it had water there, it would also have grass.

I slipped Gypsy's bridle off and hung it on the saddle horn and then stood there by her, holding the halter rope. I let the light fade for a few more minutes as Gypsy grabbed off as much grass as she could, and in the aching silence there was something good and comforting in the sounds as she snapped off the grass and chewed it down. I laid my hand along her neck and felt the ripple as she swallowed the mouthfuls of chewed hay. I always liked to do that at home, standing in the barn beside a horse just finished with his day's work, with Pa throwing the harness up on the pegs and grumbling about how low the hay was getting and saying, "Wart, did you feed the chickens and bring in the eggs?" I wished I was there now—

When Gypsy had fed for a few minutes

I decided I had better try to get a little farther up the ravine before it was full dark. We still had to make sure the water was there, higher up, and more grass. By feel more than by sight I made a short circle around her and broke off a big armload of the grass she had not had time to eat. I'd carry it with me and give it to her when we stopped.

I tightened my grip on the halter rope and gave her a jerk. She jerked back. I pulled harder. She snorted and lunged back for more grass. In the end, I got her to go by letting her smell the grass I had gathered for her, and she stumbled after me with her neck stretched out and her teeth grabbing off little wisps of the feed.

This ravine was a little more open than the first one, with places where the spring rains had washed out small, flat areas. Some of the washes had swept out a space under the overhanging rocky sides, and this is what I was looking for. With plenty of luck and just a few more minutes of this faint light I would find a place like that near the rain pool and the grass, and large enough to shelter me and my horse.

six

THIRTY YARDS UP THE RAVINE I FOUND WHAT I was looking for. I couldn't see the water—it just looked like a patch of faint, shiny black shadow under the bank of the ravine—but Gypsy smelled it and lunged forward, nearly pulling my arm out of the socket. Her head went down, and then I heard that hissing *s-s-s-sip!* sound a horse makes as it pulls in water through lips just barely open. This wasn't a spring; the water was left in the hollowed rock from the last rainstorm, and although it wasn't clean enough for me to drink, it was good enough for a horse.

Gypsy drank till I thought she'd bust, and at last raised her head, sneezed, shook herself, and then stood there like horses do, "chewing" the last bit of water and letting the water and bits of soggy grass spatter down on my boots.

I was so tired, I could have just crumpled down beside the horse, but of course that was the last thing I could let myself do. I still had a little faint light, and while it lasted I had to get myself settled for the night. Straining my eyes, I looked around. In the shadows I could make out what looked like a concave slant to the opposite wall. I hoped it would be big enough for both of us, but I had to be able to see it before I could know for sure.

I knew Pa would have put some matches in the saddlebags. He hadn't told me, and I hadn't asked, but I knew they would be there. I reached up and unbuckled the flap of the one on the right and carefully felt under the bundles of bread and ham. There was a paper sack of nails and staples, but no matches. I opened the other saddlebag and I could feel my hammer, more nails, a pair of wire-cutters, and at the bottom another towel-wrapped bundle. And there under the last bundle was the small cardboard box—matches.

My fingers were stiff with the cold already, but I peeled off my right glove and took three matches and struck them together. A quick little flame burst up—I could even feel some warmth from it—and I held the matches up and quickly looked around. Yes—on the opposite side of the ravine, maybe twenty feet from the pool of water at my feet, was an overhang of rock just tall enough for Gypsy to stand under the outer edge, and wide enough so I could fix my bedroll at the back where she wouldn't step on me.

So here it was—home sweet home for tonight.

I had to have a fire. I didn't have to cook anything, but there was no way I was going to sit here in the dark for a couple of hours and then roll up in my blankets—still in the pitch-dark—and alone. Well, I knew that having a fire wouldn't keep me from being alone, but . . . somehow when you're alone, having a fire makes it seem less . . . alone. I can't explain it. I just knew I had to have a fire. And besides that, I had another good reason for having a fire. A fire would scare off— what? Bobcat? Bear? Well, whatever it was that had caused that smear of blood to be left on the rocks. I couldn't stay up and watch all night—the fire would do that for me.

I tied Gypsy by the halter rope to a small juniper and looked around. Then, moving more by feel than anything, I located some dry brush, and what felt like a broken section of a tree trunk. I made a small pile of wood near the rocks and finally picked a spot close to the outer lip of the overhang, where I crumpled handfuls of the finest twigs. On top of them I piled the larger branches that I snapped in two over my knee. When I set a match to it, it blazed up, and even Gypsy turned around to look at it, as if the fire made her think of home. Pa says horses don't like fire, but Gypsy stood there, her ears flopping back and forth, looking at it, with tiny pinpoints of light reflecting in her eyes.

When I had the fire going pretty well, I went back along the walls of the ravine and broke off armload after armload of dry brush, and finally hauled the remains of the tree trunk up close. It looked like a lot of firewood, but I knew most of it would burn very fast, and this fire would be all I had between me and the cold and the dark. I banked the fire with a high outer wall of rocks that would hold what little heat there was under the overhang. I planned to move Gypsy pretty soon and tie her on a very short rope so she would be close to me during the night. Ordinarily in a place like this, you'd tie your horse where it could get its own grass and water, but that meant leaving her by the pool and that was too far away—even though it probably wasn't more than twenty feet. I had to make sure she was safe.

I went back then and took the rifle scabbard, blankets, canteens, and saddlebags off the saddle and brought them up near the fire. Then I took the saddle off and brought it up, too. I would use the saddle for a pillow, just like the old cowboys used to do.

Finally I was satisfied that I had done all I could to make the campsite safe. Making it comfortable didn't even enter into it. I left Gypsy by the pool for a while longer so she could drink again if she wanted to. I would bring her up close before I let myself go to sleep.

Sleep. For a second I stood there in the cold, watching the orange flicker of the fire, and thought about my bunk at home in the loft, and the way it felt crawling into it on cold nights when Ma would give me a small sack of heated salt to put down under the quilts to keep my feet warm. Right now I'd have given just about anything to be back there at the ranch house, with Davy making a racket and Ma telling me to wash my hands, and Pa yelling at me because I'd been late throwing hay into the cows' mangers. I didn't know home was so good, I thought, as I stared at the wall of cold darkness that was settling in around me.

After I put a short chunk of wood close to the fire to sit on, I opened the saddlebags and took out two more biscuits and some ham. As I ate the biscuits I heated up the ham over the fire with a stick poked through it. It didn't get very hot, but still, it tasted good. I drank a little water, but not too much, because I wouldn't get to refill the canteens until I reached the first of the real springs, and that would be sometime tomorrow.

After I finished eating I held my hand out to the fire where I could see better, and examined the cuts. They looked a little puffy, and the skin was beginning to turn red. They were sore, too. Fine, I thought. Great. By the time I got home these cuts would be so infected that it would take days or weeks for them to heal. I washed them with a little water, but that was all I could do.

Then I got up and searched around to find the best way to tether Gypsy for the night. I finally settled on a snag of rock that had the right shape. It was close enough to where I would sleep for me to feel safe about the horse, but not so close that she could step on me. Then I brought her up from the pool, bribing her to move with two handfuls of grass, and at last had her where I wanted her. I tied the rope fairly short so she couldn't wrap it around her neck or one of her legs. She coughed a couple of times, smelled the ground, and relaxed. She was settled for the night.

By now the outer wall of my fireplace had collapsed a little, and as I found stones to fill the gaps I got to thinking about rocks, and the rock-throwing fights we used to have at school. The teacher used to yell at us for it, but we did it anyway. Me and Roscoe Bailey and Tom Fenway used to team up against Lije Bennett and Rob Thompson and Aaron Moss. We were pretty well matched, though—nobody ever really won. When we got tired of throwing rocks, we'd throw the bull. Brag about riding rough horses, killing rattlesnakes, working like men at haying or roundup—anything we could think of. Next time I saw Roscoe or Tom I would be sure to just happen to mention this trip. Not that there was anything unusual for any of us to be sent out after livestock, but it was always easier to bring in the cattle. I would make sure they knew it was horses I was after and that it took me two days. I sure hoped I would be able to tell them that I brought them in, too. I would have to tell the truth if I talked about it, though, no matter how it turned out. Especially if I talked to Tom. Tom either knows stuff I don't know, or else he just figures it out faster than I do.

At last, I ran out of things to do. I was still hungry and thirsty but I couldn't use up any more of my food and water, so there was nothing to do but sleep. I had put off going to sleep as long as I could because I knew that once I tried to lie down and roll up in my blankets— close to the fire and with Gypsy stamping and asleep on her feet nearby—there would no longer be any way to keep from thinking about . . . whatever it was that had attacked the horses. And about the fact that I was out here with nothing much between me and it but the fire and a lightweight .22 rifle. Of the two, the fire was going to protect me the most, because a .22 wouldn't stop anything big, even if I could hit it—and I wasn't all that sure I could shoot straight, especially in the dark, and scared half to death.

And finally I lay down on my bed of sand, my head on the saddle and the blankets rolled around me, and as I looked up at the rocky ceiling, I let my mind go to work on it.

I asked myself questions: What could make a wound on a horse?

Had to be an animal. Horses don't run into rocks and trees.

What could make a wound that big?

Had to be a big animal. Bobcat? No, too small. Wouldn't attack a horse. Bear? Could be, although bears don't often try to take something as big as a horse. Besides, bears should be fat and sleepy this time of year, about ready to den up.

And that left . . . cougar.

A cougar is big, strong, fast, and hungry. Cougars don't den up in the winter. And a hungry cougar will attack anything. Cattle. Horses. Deer. People . . .

Gypsy snorted and raised her head suddenly. I exploded up out of my blankets, my heart pounding as I reached for the rifle. With my finger on the trigger I searched the darkness but couldn't see anything. Then I heard, icy and cold but comforting, the call of a coyote above me on the ridge. Just a coyote.

I pulled some big wood onto the fire and then rolled my blankets around me again and lay back down, with my right hand on the rifle. Sleep, I told myself. Even if there is a cougar out there—especially if there is a cougar out there—I've got to get some sleep.

I was glad at least that I'd chosen this campsite in the ravine, with a solid wall at my back and only two directions—up the ravine and down—for something to come at me.

I guess I had slept maybe a couple of hours when Gypsy began to kick up another fuss. I woke up and rolled over, my hand reaching for the rifle as naturally as if I'd been doing this all my life.

The fire had burned down till there were only a few tiny orange coals. It was very dark, but when I leaned out and looked up I could see that the clouds were broken and the moon shone through them like weak lamplight through a window. It was only a half-moon. Even if it had been clear, it wouldn't have helped me see much.

But I could hear, and I knew Gypsy was snorting and dancing and straining on her rope—I had better get to her before she broke it and took off. I slid out of my blankets and, with the rifle in my left hand, I felt along the overhang to where Gypsy's rope was fastened. I found the rope and, with my hand on it so it wouldn't trip me, I moved carefully toward the horse, talking softly to her as I approached.

"Ho, Gypsy. Ho, Gypsy. Take it easy. I'm here. Ho, girl. Ho, girl. Good girl. Good girl. Easy now"—My hand slid up the rope to where it was tied with a bowline knot to the ring in her halter, and then I reached on up to rub her head behind the ears. Gypsy liked that, and besides, I thought she would feel better now that I was awake and standing there with her to face whatever had frightened her. She was still snorting and trying to pick up scent from the air, but at last she stood still beside me.

There—that big shape by the pool—was that a light-colored rock? Or a cougar? And down farther—was that a dun-colored hide moving silently in and out of the willows? Or grass, bending in the light wind?

Sometimes in very dim light you can see something better if you look just to the left or right of it. I don't know why this is so, but it works. I tried it now, and I could see that what I thought might be a cougar was nothing but rocks and patches of dry, tall grass. Gypsy was quiet now, too, and that made me feel there wasn't any real threat, at least not now. Gypsy could just as easily have spooked if she'd heard a rabbit loping along down the ravine, or if she'd scented a skunk or another coyote out scouring the ridge for that same rabbit. With a horse, a little scare can be just as much excuse to bolt as a big one. It's one of the things that makes living with horses so interesting—you don't have a lot of time on your hands to use up sleeping or just taking it easy.

At last I decided that whatever had scared her was gone. I checked the knots in her rope, and then leaned the rifle against a big rock while I pulled in a few big heavy sticks, together with some dry twigs, and laid them over the bed of coals. The dry twigs caught and in a few seconds were blazing up. Then the heavier pieces began to smolder. I knew it would burn for at least a couple of hours more.

I took one last look around, and then

lay down, rifle beside me, and closed my eyes. Sleep, dammit. I had to . . . sleep. . . .

But I woke up again, and I guess it must have been around midnight. I was so cold, I felt as if I would never move again, and when I rolled over to look at the fire, I could see it was almost out. It was pure torture to crawl out of my blankets, but I forced myself to do it, and pretty soon I had the fire blazing again. I checked Gypsy—she was dozing on her feet—and got myself a drink of water from the canteen. I was still only half awake as I put the canteen down by the big split rock and headed back to my blankets.

Then, just as I leaned over to pick up the blanket so I could roll myself up in it, I heard Pa say, "Always check yourself."

Slowly I turned around. There, by the big split rock, was the canteen I had just put down. The canteen had slipped over, the cap was loose, and the water was dripping onto the ground. And it was all the water I had left.

I went over to the canteen and screwed the cap on tight. Pa, I thought, I'm out here all by myself, but you're still following me.

And as that thought came to me, I whirled and looked all around. Could he be here? Could he really have followed me?

But there was no lean, hard man walking toward me through the darkness. No dark face under a dark hat, no heavy hand or harsh voice. God, how I wished he was there to say, "Wart, you damn fool—Wart, how many times do I have to tell you to watch out—Wart—Wart—Wart—" I went back and rolled the blankets tight around me.

Wart. That's what he calls me. I guess that's what he thinks I am—a wart. A nuisance. A bump on his finger that he can't get rid of. He started calling me that when I was real little, when I was always falling down and making mistakes. Like falling into the water trough, eating green apples, opening and closing gates wrong so I let the chickens out and the coyotes got them, and kept the cows in so they didn't get out to pasture. Pa used to haul me into the house when I was only five or six years old and beg Ma to keep me in—he couldn't get around fast enough to fix all the stuff I messed up. I grew up and got smarter, but I guess he never noticed. Anyway, he still calls me Wart.

Ma doesn't always call me Wart. And she doesn't like it much when Pa calls me Wart. But then I don't like it when Ma calls me by my real name either.

I guess Pa and Ma had an awful fight when I was born because Ma insisted on naming me after Pa's father, and after Pa, too. Pa's father was one of the early pioneers in this country, and Ma was real proud to have married into his family. As long as I can remember I've heard stories about how my grandpa had driven a team and wagon in the wagon train when his family made the long trek from Ohio to the Oregon country in 1857. Grandpa was only twelve years old then—the same age I am now—and he used to tell his kids, and then tell me when I was old enough, stories about the crossing. He told about the ferry that took the wagons across the Mississippi and how the captain of the boat made them pay before they got on the boat so they wouldn't get across and then tell him they didn't have any money. Somebody had tried that on him, thinking he would just leave them on the west side of the river so they could go on to Oregon, Grandpa said, but the captain had his hired men put the wagon back onto the ferry and he took them back to the Missouri side and left them there. I guess that ferryboat captain died rich.

And Grandpa told us about some of the people coming out to Oregon who had brought nice dishes, and mahogany rockers, and gold-framed mirrors in their wagons, thinking to haul them all the way to the new homes they were going to build, and how they had had to throw them out along the way when the horses wore out and the wagons broke down.

He told us about the horses and cattle that sickened and died, and how he and the other kids passed the time counting skeletons of dead animals along the way.

And they counted graves, too. Sometimes the graves were so shallow, the wolves dug up the corpses and ate them; and sometimes the graves were neat with high piles of stones to keep the wolves out. Some of the graves were unmarked, but some had wooden crosses with names painted onto or burnt into the wood— ALICE MAYBERRY, AGED 32. DIED JUNE 13, 1857, OF CHOLERA. Or JOSHUA FULTON, AGED 21, KILT BY INDIANS, AUG. 9, 1856. Sometimes it was just OUR BABY. SMITH. 1854. Grandpa said nobody needed a map to follow the road to Oregon. All they had to do was follow the line of graves. His own mother died near the Robidoux Pass, and he still had a piece of the wood his father had used to make the cross for her grave. He had whittled a hole in the little piece of wood and he wore it on his watch chain after he got old enough to buy a watch. That piece of wood was buried with him, but before he died he gave his watch to my pa to keep for me because I am the oldest grandson. The ranch came from Grandpa also, because two of his older sons died, and his daughters married men who took them back East to live, so my pa was the one to take the ranch over.

Grandpa told us to work hard and pay our bills and pray every day and watch out that we never put green hay into the barn. But he never told us where an Irishman whose family came from County Kilarney got a name like Horace Fernando Nolan.

Ma named me John—after my pa— and Fernando after his father. I guess it's no wonder Pa calls me Wart. . . .

seven

As I lay there looking out from under the overhang I could see that the clouds were still broken. I wondered if tomorrow would be clearer or if the weather would close in again. The thing about weather is that you can't do anything about it. You just take what comes. A lot of things are like that.

I never liked either of my names, but then nobody ever asked me. When you're a kid other people decide things for you. Like Pa decided I had to go after the horses yesterday. So many things a kid has to do— or to go to—that he doesn't want to do . . .

Like last summer, when I hadn't wanted to go to the wedding. I didn't care whether Miss Penneyman, the bride, got married or not; she was the schoolteacher who had rapped my knuckles with a ruler for not paying attention. The only good thing about this wedding was that she wouldn't be teaching school anymore.

And as if it had happened only last week, I could remember sitting at the back of the wagon that day in June, on the way to her wedding at the schoolhouse. I was way too much dressed up to be comfortable, and I was itchy and grouchy as I sat with my feet dangling out the back of the wagon.

Pa had put the good black harness on Pet and Snip, and even wiped the leather straps down with a rag dabbed with neat's-foot oil. The silver studs on the harness sparkled as the horses, fresh roached and groomed, tossed their heads when a rabbit sprang out of the way, or a coyote barked somewhere near. Pet and Snip seemed to be walking with a little snap to their gait, as if they were proud to be taking the family to the wedding.

I wondered if the horses really felt that way, or if I only imagined. It seemed as if everybody and his cat was excited about this wedding—everybody but me. Pa had put on a bow tie and a vest—it was too warm for a coat—and Ma had squeezed Davy into his best pants and shirt even though they were a little too small for him now. Ma wore a ripply blue dress trimmed with a wide creamy lace collar, and the full skirt of the dress just brushed the tops of her black button shoes. There had been a few quiet whispers between Pa and Ma about "Do I show much yet?" and Pa saying, "No—no—not at all. You look like a regular princess." Pa and Ma almost acted as if it were their wedding, or that they had some part in it that I couldn't see. . . .

When we got to the schoolhouse, the yard around it was cluttered with wagons and buggies, and horses unhitched and tethered to fence posts, trees, and the wheels of the wagons they had pulled. There was a buzz of talk, and people were everywhere—women in colored dresses not faded from working in ranch house kitchens; children in hand-me-downs but with their hair braided or curled with egg whites, and the boys' combed and slicked down with some of their Pa's brilliantine. The men mostly wore ties and vests with their best work pants, a few had coats, and all had hats, but then no self-respecting man would be caught outside without his hat on. I had mine on, too, even though it was old and faded. There's a certain age when a kid stops being a kid, and then he has to wear a hat. I wore a hat.

But the main thing I saw—and Pa saw it at the same time—was the automobile. It sat a little to the north of the school-house, under a shady locust tree, and all the men who had managed to get away from their wives were crowded around it. The women were clumped over near the door of the schoolhouse, and some of them looked real put out about the auto-mobile and the men gathered there.

I started to head in the direction of the automobile, but Pa stopped me. "Wart— help me unhitch."

Pet and Snip had never been unhitched from the wagon that fast. Pa unhooked Pet's tugs from her doubletree, and I did

Snip's, and in seconds we had the latches off the wagon tongue and hooked up on the collar pegs. Then Pa led the team around to the side of the wagon, tied Pet to the front wheel and Snip to the back wheel. He kept looking back over his shoulder at the automobile, but then he went to help Ma down.

Davy had already jumped down and taken off like a rabbit. I saw him disappear among the men around the automobile. When the horses were tied, I followed him. Pa was late in getting to the crowd around the auto—he walked Ma over to where the other women stood and then, as she melted in among them, he raised his hat and turned back to where all the men were. In a minute I saw him shove into an inner row, no more than an arm's length from the front end of the thing. I threw off all the manners Pa and Ma had taught me and elbowed my way up to where he stood. I was so close, I could smell—whatever the smell was—and see my face reflected in the shiny black metal.

The auto had high, narrow wheels, with rubber tires and flimsy spokes, an open seat padded like a sofa, and there was a steering *wheel* where the driver would sit. There were levers with knobs and levers without knobs. There was a kind of hinged lid on the front, and somebody—the owner, I guess—raised the lid and folded it back so we could see the engine.

I've seen lots of steam engines, and Pa has told me how they work. There's a firebox, and the tank for water, and the long belts that carry the power, and the gauges and flywheels and all that. This didn't look anything like that; in fact, it looked like a pile of junk, but of course we knew it wasn't. The man by the engine took a little stick and pointed out what he called pistons. A carburetor. Spark plugs. Reverse pedal. Brake pedal. Then somebody said, "Granger—how does the damn thing work?" And the man with the stick showed how the gasoline—from that tank down there—was pumped up through here—to here—to fire in the pistons that made something revolve, sending power to the wheels so they would start to turn, moving the whole thing forward at a speed of—oh, maybe as much as twenty-five miles per hour! *Twenty-five miles per hour!*

I felt somebody pushing in beside me and I started to push back, but when I looked around it was Tom Fenway. I grunted, and Tom grunted, but we had no time for each other. We couldn't waste a second of this—we'd probably never get another chance to see an automobile. It did cross my mind that if I'd known this thing would be at the wedding, I'd have been ready to come an hour earlier.

When it was finally time for the wedding to start, someone said, "The Penney-mans are here," but none of the men even looked up. The women all raised some excitement, talking about the long white dress and the lace veil, but finally the wives had to come over and drag their husbands away from the automobile. Ma grabbed Davy and me and then took Pa's arm, and we all followed along as the crowd moved into the schoolhouse.

There wasn't much room inside, because the desks were still bolted in place, but some people stood the littlest kids on the desks, and that made more room. Then an old lady in a purple dress and a black hat with long white feathers marched up the aisle and sat down at the old foot-pump organ. Ma had told me the difference between the two wedding marches, humming them for me, and I recognized this as the "going in" one. Pa and Ma were standing just in front of me, and Ma was leaning a little against him.

Then we heard the doors squeak open behind us, and a kind of rippled silence went over the room. Then I saw the preacher, Mr. Harrington, in a black suit, come walking slowly up the aisle. After him came two women in fancy, ruffly dresses, carrying little bouquets of pink roses. Last came the bride, Miss Penneyman, holding the arm of some man, very old, who walked as if his legs hurt.

"Who's that ol' man?" I whispered.

"Her uncle, Joshua Penneyman," said Ma softly. "Her father's dead, so he's going to give her away."

Give her away? I liked that idea. I never liked Miss Penneyman anyway.

The last person to walk up the aisle was the man Miss Penneyman was to marry. Pa had said his name was Elijah Blackwood. He was older than Miss Penneyman, tall and heavy-shouldered, and a rancher—you could tell that from his bowed legs and his weathered face. He was dressed up, too, in a black coat and tan pants, shiny black boots, and a bow tie with the ends hanging down. His hair was black, and it looked like he had combed it down with brilliantine, too.

Then all the marchers were past me. There were footsteps, whispers, a few muttered words, but as far as the wedding was concerned, I didn't see any of it. It didn't matter—all I could think about was the automobile. How much did it cost? Was it hard to learn to drive? Would—oh, God—would I ever live to see Pa own one—would I ever own one myself?

All at once I noticed that the "going out" song was wheezing out of the old organ. I craned my neck, and, yes, there they came. Miss Penneyman—no, Mrs. Blackwood now—arm in arm with her new husband,

and all the others following after them. As they came down the aisle, people stepped in behind them and made a long train of people going out. Everybody was smiling, but I saw tears on some of the women's faces, and others had handkerchiefs handy. I looked up at Ma, and she was smiling— but at Pa, not at the bride. I wondered why she was smiling, but by that time we were all outside again, and I forgot about Ma and Pa and stood there looking over at the automobile again. The men all went over to shake hands with Mr. Blackwood and tip their hats to the new bride, but as soon as they could get away, they all sidled back over to the automobile.

The women saw them getting away, so right off they began fixing a table and loading it with boxes and baskets of food they had brought. Ma had brought a basket, too, with one of her peach upside-down cakes and some homemade pickles and jams.

Then Tom came up to me. "Come on! He's going to show us how you start it!"

I turned and joined the stampede. I

knew I might never get a chance like this again.

The owner—Sam Granger, the banker from Princeville—reached in under the seat of the auto and took out a piece of iron bar bent into a funny shape. It had a short end, then a right angle at about ten inches, and it right-angled again a few inches farther along into something that looked like a handle or a grip. Granger went to the front of the automobile, leaned over, and fitted one end of the metal bar into a hole in the front end. Then he began to make sharp, hard turns of the metal bar.

Everybody waited. Nothing happened.

More turns of the bar. I looked at Tom, and he looked at me. We had no idea what Granger was doing, or what would happen.

More turns.

Granger was starting to sweat.

"Need some help, Granger?" came a voice from the back of the crowd.

Granger clenched his teeth. Sweat was trickling down his face. I felt like I was doing the turning myself. I wanted it to happen—

—Whatever it was.

Then suddenly a *pop-pop-bang-pop!* exploded from under the black hood. The whole crowd of men sank back and then closed in again. Tom and I were elbowed and kicked all over again. But we both got our hands on that jiggling, dancing, shaking, banging, popping, *hot* black hood. And we heard, close up and smoking and stinking, the first gasoline engine that ever spoiled a wedding.

I stood there with my hand on the black shiny metal. And all at once I understood something. The older men—Pa, Tom's pa, and the others—would be the first to see these machines close up, and maybe even use them. But kids like Tom and me—we would be the ones whose whole lives might be lived with tractors and automobiles—maybe even other machines that hadn't been invented yet. It would be Tom and other kids like him that I would go forward into my life with—not Pa.

There was only one other thing about the wedding that I still remembered after all these months. It happened while Pa and Ma were dancing a waltz. I was full of fried chicken and coconut cake and lemonade, and was sitting over by the fiddlers. I just happened to look up as Pa and Ma went by me in a slow turn. And Pa, ever so gently and quickly, like the brush of a bird's wing, bent his head and kissed Ma on the cheek. No one else saw them. . . .

I pretended I didn't see either. Maybe it wasn't just *this* wedding that they were celebrating today. . . .

And when the wedding was over, and all the food eaten, and the fiddlers quit playing, and Sam Granger cranked up his automobile and drove it off in a cloud of smoke and noise, we all hitched up our horses again, and one by one the wagons and buggies rolled away from the schoolhouse.

I rode at the back of our wagon again, watching the road going backward toward the passing day. Pet and Snip were glad to be heading home, and their hooves made a nice, brisk drum on the road. Davy was asleep on a blanket in the wagon bed, and

Ma and Pa sat close together on the wagon seat, their shoulders touching, but not saying much.

And as I sat there feeling every pounding jolt of the iron-rimmed wheels, I remembered that I hadn't wanted to go to this wedding. Had felt it was a waste of time. But now I had this hazy kind of feeling that a lot had happened, even if not much of it had to do with the wedding. There was the automobile, the feeling of going forward with Tom, and Pa kissing Ma in the dance. It had been a kind of magic day, a look into the future—and maybe the past—and somehow I felt as if I had changed, though nothing had really happened to me.

Now as I lay there in the cold and the dark, I felt sleep finally coming close again. And maybe, I thought, maybe someday I'll feel the same way about today, about Pa sending me after the horses, that I had felt about the wedding.

And then I slept again.

eight

WHEN DAYBREAK FINALLY CAME I WOKE UP knowing I didn't want to be here. After one quick look to see that the clouds had closed in solid, I lay for a while with my eyes shut. For a couple of minutes I thought about just staying right where I was for the rest of the day, and then riding home in the late afternoon and telling Pa I couldn't find the horses. He wouldn't know—no one would ever know—that I hadn't gone on and searched for them for the rest of the day. I thought about how my legs had hurt last night after riding all day, and how scared I had been when I'd seen the smear of blood and then how scared I was during the night. Maybe Pa could come back with me in a day or so, when Ma would be able to stay alone, and we could catch the horses then. I told myself that it would work—that they wouldn't follow Ol' Rosie off into the mountains, of course not—and everything would be fine. . . .

But hard as I tried, I couldn't get myself to swallow all that malarkey about the horses being okay for another day or two, and me and Pa being able to catch up with them. And finally I realized that I was thinking about quitting and running for home because I was thinking with my head under the covers and my eyes shut. And whenever I do that, I get bad ideas.

Like the time when I decided I would run away from home. I'd made that plan before I got up in the morning, too, with my head under the blankets and my eyes shut. Pa had thrashed me the day before for doing something dumb—I had left the gate to the chicken yard open, and we lost some good hens to the coyotes. Pa was fit to be tied, and he really let me have it. I knew I'd let the chickens out—even though I wouldn't admit it—but I thought Pa was mean to punish me so hard. So the next day I made this plan, and I got a big red bandana and put a biscuit and an apple into it and tied it up—that was going to be my food to eat until I got someplace where I could "get a job." I was about eight years old at the time, and I don't know exactly who I thought was going to hire me, but I wasn't worried about that. So I waited till Ma and Pa got busy, and I slipped off. I started down the road toward—where? The closest ranch to ours is seven miles away, and the people who run it are Swedes, and the general store is over fifteen miles away. But I guess I wasn't thinking about any of that.

I got maybe a mile down the wagon road from home and I began to get scared. I'd never been this far from Ma and Pa in my life. I started looking into the brush and seeing wolves and bears, and probably cougars and rattlesnakes and maybe lions and tigers, too. Then it began to cloud up, and I got cold because I'd forgotten to bring a coat. I started to bawl.

When a rabbit jumped out of the brush beside me I hopped up in the air, and when I came down I turned and lit out for home and Ma and Pa as fast as I could run. And there came Trixie tearing down the road after me, and behind her, on the big saddle horse, Socks, was Pa.

"Wart!" yelled Pa. "What the hell you doin' way out here?"

I wanted to scream and holler, but I was choking it in. "I'm—I'm—"

"Are you runnin' away?" thundered Pa.

I looked up at him. Pa's face was white—not red, the way it gets when he's mad—and all at once I knew I was finally headed in the right direction. And I figured out what to say: "Hell, no, Pa. I'm runnin' *home*—"

And then, instead of letting me ride behind him on the horse, he made me walk all the way home for *cussing*—

Now at last my eyes opened, there in the cold morning and on that sandy bed, as if they had decided to do it whether I wanted them to open or not. I lay there for a minute looking up at the rocks leaning out over me, and I thought about my eyes and how they seemed to take charge of opening and seeing all by themselves, as if they knew what had to be done and they did it. I guess maybe lots of things happen that way. It's not like you get many choices to do—or not do—something. You do it because it has to be done.

Like Ma having the baby, no matter how much it hurt.

Like Pa plowing in a freezing wind and doing chores before daybreak, when he has to break the ice in the water troughs so the animals can drink.

Like my having to go on and find those lousy horses no matter if I was cold or tired or hungry or scared.

All at once I remember what I'd said to Pa, that someday there would be machines to do some of the work that horses do now. I figured there were probably more automobiles besides Granger's out here in eastern Oregon, although I hadn't seen any but his. And someday maybe there would be machines to cut hay and harvest wheat, not just thresh it with steam engines, and to haul crops in from the fields and pull plows and harrows and drills. And if we had some of those machines—

I'd still have to get out of a warm bed and help Pa. All the same, I bet an automobile wouldn't kick you or throw off its saddle blanket or bite you. . . .

Well, even if Henry Ford was making great automobiles back East somewhere, and the tractor companies were putting big, noisy coal and gasoline engines together with their flywheels and gears and stuff, none of that was going to help me now.

I peeled the blankets back and crawled out into air that was so cold, it seemed to burn my face. And as I stood there, hunched over, shivering and almost ready to cut and run for home, I got a nice surprise present, but one of those presents you don't really want: A big white snowflake came floating down out of the sky and landed on the back of my hand.

"Lord," I said half out loud as I pushed

my last dry branches into the nearly dead fire and helped them catch fire with a match, "tell me it isn't going to snow. Tell me it isn't going to snow all day. *Tell* me."

But I ate two biscuits and toasted a slice of ham over the fire and ate that, and drank some water, and all the time the snowflakes kept drifting down. It was almost enough to make me hope the school board could find a new schoolteacher and open the school again. I never liked school all that much, but you don't have to read George Washington's inaugural address outside in the snow.

I repacked my saddlebags, shook out my blankets and rolled them, and even got some dry grass and rubbed Gypsy down, and all the time I wanted it to stop snowing, but it didn't. Finally, after Gypsy had finished eating the grass I pulled for her, I untied her and led her down to the rain pool for a long drink of water, and there, out from under the rock overhang, I could see better. I didn't much like what I saw.

Because I couldn't see anything. Falling

snow is like a heavy screen. You can see through rain, but snow is solid, and it cuts you off from landmarks and even directions, if you aren't careful. There have been blizzards in this country in the last few years that were so bad, people got lost on familiar land close to their home and froze to death. One year Pa tied ropes together and then tied one end to a nail by the kitchen door and the other end to the barn door so he could hold on to the rope and go out and feed and water the stock, and not get lost.

Around me now the rocks were beginning to hold a coating of white, and the ground was turning a dirty gray that would soon be white also. Gypsy's tracks down from the overhang were the only clear marks I could see.

And suddenly I took another look at her tracks. Hellfire, the snow falling now was going to make it hard—no, impossible— for me to pick up the trail of the horses—

I had the saddle on Gypsy in record time. Kicked her twice to make her let out air, cinched it down tight, and slapped on the saddlebags, rolled and tied the ropes, canteens, blankets, and rifle scabbard so fast, I only wished Pa could have seen me.

But he would just have said, "Hell, Wart—what took you so long?"

nine

TWO HOURS LATER ON THE CREST OF THE HIGH ridge, I pulled Gypsy in to blow and rest. I hadn't seen hide nor hair of a horse except the one I was riding, and I hadn't been able to pick up any tracks—the snow was just deep enough to cover them. I had searched one more ravine, a steep cleft full of loose rocks and dead brush, and as I came back down it after making sure it was empty, a rock had turned under Gypsy's left hind foot—the one that already had the barbwire cuts on it. She staggered, and her hindquarters went out from under her.

I rolled out of the saddle but by the time I hit the ground, she had caught herself. I stood there by her for a minute, and my hand holding the reins was shaking. What if she had really fallen—maybe broken a leg? The last thing in this world I wanted to do now was walk home from here and tell Pa I'd ruined a horse.

Slowly I worked my way around in front of her, almost afraid to look, and smoothed my right hand back over her neck, her flank, and down over the hind leg. Gypsy was snorting and shaking, too, and she turned her head to look hard at her leg. It was a bad sign. But as I ran my hand down the leg I couldn't feel any breaks and no cuts from the sharp edge of the rock. Maybe—maybe I would be lucky this time and she just lost her balance and didn't really do any damage.

Then Gypsy caught sight of a clump of grass a couple of yards away, and she jerked the reins and moved over to where she could get at it. I watched her carefully, but she seemed to move all right.

I can't take her into any more of these rocky places, I told myself. I'll have to get off and search them on foot. It'll take longer, but I can't risk her taking a fall.

I let her rest for maybe ten minutes, eating all the grass she could find, and hoped it would make her feel better. Then I led her down and out of the ravine. Got to get moving, I said to myself. And I got to stop making mistakes.

And now as I sat there high on the steep flank of the ridge, I took a long, hard look around. So far the snowfall had stayed light enough that I could see pretty good for at least one hundred yards in any direction, even though I couldn't pick up tracks on the ground right under me. But I hadn't heard anything either—and if you're anywhere near a band of horses, you'll hear a whinny, or a cough, or one of their long, rattly sneezes. So I was sure the horses were still ahead of me. But *where?* There was one more deep ravine to search, and then after that the big ridge broke up into several square miles of jumbled rocks, little hills, and draws, all of it covered with heavy juniper and pine forest. If the horses were in there—and I was just about certain by now that they were—it was going to be one rotten job finding them and then getting them out. Gypsy was a slow old horse, already tired, and I was chasing ten animals who were rested and fresh and drunk on the idea that they had run off. I could run them around in these hills for a week and they could always stay ahead of me.

There was just one—no, two—good chances to catch them. I might get them into the last ravine and close it off quick with ropes and brush, or I might be able to shut them in around the farthest spring. Pa had started to put something like a small corral fence around the spring some years back but had never finished it. It wouldn't be easy to rope off the gap in the fence before they saw me and stampeded through it, but I might be able to pull it off if I could move fast enough. If I could get them into either of the two places, I would have a chance. Like Pa said, I had to get them penned up long enough to get lead ropes on Pet and Snip, and then some of the other horses—except Ol' Rosie—would be likely to follow as I led the team home. Pet was the horse they would follow, and she was gentle and quiet. She kind of reminded me of those ladies at the wedding—the one who played the organ, and the ones who served the food and saw to it that everything got done right.

So why did the whole rotten band of horses—including Pet—take off with Ol' Rosie every once in a while? Well, I don't know. Nobody else knows either, and that's what makes it so hard to work with horses. You just don't go out and start them up like a tractor and they work all day without any trouble. You never know when they'll come up with some crazy idea of their own. That's why Pa had said he hoped he never saw Ol' Rosie again. So did I. The best thing that could happen now, as far as I was concerned, would be for me to find all the horses except Ol' Rosie and just take them home, peaceful and civilized and quiet. I really hoped it would work out that way.

Well, five minutes or so had gone by now, and Gypsy would be rested. I kicked my heels into her sides and lifted her reins, signaling her to get started.

Gypsy swung her head down and snorted.

I kicked.

She kicked. Left hind foot.

I tapped her flanks with the ends of the reins.

She kicked again. Left hind foot again. And then she turned and "pointed" at it with her muzzle.

I looked down. Oh, hell.

Gypsy was standing on three feet, with her left hind hoof tilted on the rim. And above the hoof and up into the cannon was a thick, spongy swelling. The fall in the ravine had done it.

Gypsy had gone lame.

I climbed down off the horse. For a minute I just stood there beside her. Then I leaned over and laid my face in the hollow where her neck and shoulder met. Her rough winter coat felt warm against my cheek, but all the rest of me was cold, tired and numb. I could feel tears starting even though I bit my lip to stop them.

God Almighty, I thought. Would you look at me. Miles from home, in a snow-storm, and my horse has gone lame. I know I shouldn't have let it happen, but I was trying to push—to get this job done. And no matter how hard I pushed, I still haven't caught up with the horses. Haven't even seen them—haven't so much as a clue where they are out here in these rocks and gullies.

I stood there for a couple minutes more, wondering how I would explain all this to Pa. I don't think Pa has ever made a mis-take in his life. Unless you count me . . .

Gypsy tossed her head up and down two or three times, coughed, chewed her bit, sneezed, switched her tail, and rattled her bit again. After that she tried kicking at me with her lame foot two or three times and finally got the distance figured and managed to catch me a real good clanger on my right shin. Then she swung her head around and gave me a long, innocent look out of her big onyx-colored eyes. There were snowflakes on her black eyelashes. Then finally she got tired of standing there and shrugged me off and limped forward to bite off a clump of bunchgrass just in front of her. No matter who's at fault when things get screwed up, you don't get a whole lot of sympathy from a horse. A horse will kick you, and then when you're lying there on the ground— in a pile of manure—he will walk on you before you can get up. Whoever it was who said, "A horse—a horse—my kingdom for a horse!" couldn't have had much real estate to offer for a trade.

Well, hell. I could stand here all day on the steep side of the ridge with the snow drifting down on me while I felt sorry for myself, or I could try to make the nearest cover. Up ahead was a pine tree that had no low boughs; there was enough room under it for Gypsy and me to be out of the snow, and the ground was dry, too.

I gathered the reins and stepped out ahead, pulling Gypsy along behind me. It was like pulling a battleship over dry land. Gypsy braced her three good legs, clamped her teeth on the bit, swung her rear end from side to side, and laid her ears back— always a good sign that a horse is getting ready to massacre you. I pulled, yanked, groaned, gritted my teeth, and pulled harder, and finally blew up and kicked her in the belly. Like magic, Gypsy's ears came up, her three good legs started working, and she staggered after me across the slick, snow-covered slope. Lurching and stumbling through the falling snow, we made it to the pine tree.

Quickly I tied her halter rope around the trunk of the tree and slipped the bridle off. Gypsy coughed again and made another try at kicking me, but this time I was watching and jumped back.

There was a big, smooth boulder under the tree, so I sat down on it and tried to think what to do. Or actually I tried to think what Pa would tell me to do if he was here. I could hear his voice clear as day: "You damn fool, Wart! You shouldn't have taken this old mare into that ravine where there were loose rocks for her to stumble on!"

Yeah, Pa.

Pa again: "Now you got to walk and lead her—an' you still haven't got the horses!"

Yeah, Pa. I know.

Pa: "Well, dammit, the least you could do is wrap something around her leg to hold the swelling down—"

Wrap it? With *what?*

And then I thought—with one of the towels in the saddlebags. Tear it in strips and wrap the sprain to support it.

Son of a gun. I'm smarter than I thought.

I went over and unfastened the saddle-bags and lifted them down off the saddle. I realized that I had never really examined them to see what all was in them. Maybe I could reroll some of the stuff and come up with one towel, whichever seemed the oldest and most worn out, and tear it in strips to use for bandages. The towels were made out of old flour sacks, and by the time they'd been used for a long time you could tear them fairly easy. I opened the first bag, and it held the hammer, staples, nails in a paper bag, and one towel that I had wrapped some of the remaining biscuits in. I opened the other saddlebag. On top was a very small bundle containing the last two slices of fried ham and two more biscuits. I laid it down, careful not to let it unwind. Now underneath the top bundle I saw another towel wrapped around something else. I pulled it out—surprised at how heavy it was—and unwrapped the towel.

It was a pint jar of Ma's canned peaches.

I must have sat there for nearly a minute staring at the jar. I couldn't believe it. Pa—he had told me I couldn't have any of them. And yet he had found this one small jar and put it in without telling me.

He must have known I wouldn't find it until I had eaten most of the biscuits and ham, until I was just about to the bottom of the barrel, and running out of food, nerve, and ideas.

And then, just for one split second I got a flash of how Pa must have felt, to have to send a dumb, half-baked kid like me off alone to do a hard, dangerous, important job that really needed two good men. Grown men. It must have driven him wild. . . .

Then sitting there in the cold and the silence of the falling snow, I suddenly realized that Pa had known even before he sent me what could happen out here. He knew the fence would almost surely be down, and hard to fix. He knew horses could go lame. He had known I might fail to bring the horses in. But he sent me anyway. You talk about guts. . . .

But then I stopped thinking about Pa. I had to think about me—and what would keep me going. I banged the top of the jar on the rock beside me to loosen it, and twisted the lid off. The smell of those sweet peaches came right up into my face—the smell of summer and warm sunlight and Ma in the hot kitchen boiling the jars in a big copper clothes boiler and singing "Amazing Grace" and yelling at me to bring in more wood—

I grabbed up a sharp-pointed twig and speared the chunks of peach, one by one, and ate them, and I have never in my life tasted anything so good. Slowly, tasting every single drop, I drank the juice. Then I put the jar back into the saddlebag and finally washed my hands and face with snow.

What a difference. I felt like I could handle anything now—lame horse, run-away horses, cougar. Anything.

ten

AFTER I TORE UP THE OLD TOWEL AND BANDAGED Gypsy's sprain, there was nothing to do but walk and lead her. And there was one good thing about walking: I was close to the ground. I picked up the tracks of the runaway horses in less than half an hour. They weren't too easy to see, with the light layer of snow over them, and I probably would have missed them if I'd still been riding. I followed the tracks for another half hour, moving at a snail's pace, and with plenty of halts for Gypsy to rest, and finally we crossed the last deep ravine. This time I didn't take Gypsy up the ravine but tied her to a tree on the far bank, after crossing it at the easiest place. I knew it wouldn't take much more to lame her so bad she wouldn't move at all. While she was busy trying to scratch her bridle off against the tree trunk, I pulled a big pile of bunchgrass for her to eat. That should keep her happy while I hiked up the ravine.

Although I had been sure they were up in the juniper and pine beyond the ridge, I could see now that the horses had gone up the ravine. I figured they had been looking for water again and prayed they were still there. There was a good, deep rain pool here about halfway up to the hogback that closes the upper end, and when I reached it I could see that they had been here—maybe as recently as two or three hours ago. The tracks were blurred by the snow and by them going back and forth, but I saw one or two that I knew were Ol' Rosie's, and the manure they had dropped was still fresh. But no live horses.

There was a little water trickling down into the pool from the higher rocks, and I tried to get some of it to dribble into one of my canteens, but it was hard to reach and I only got a couple of cupfuls. I had to lean out over the pool to get it and I was afraid of falling into the icy water. Wet clothes, added to what I already had—a lame horse and a long way to go—could easily be the end of me. Well, Ma says the Bible tells us that man is born to trouble. . . .

By the time I got back to Gypsy she had eaten all her grass and was looking around for more. I wished I had some grain to give her, but she'd just have to go on short rations till we got back to the ranch. Actually, of course, we were still *on* the ranch—had never left it—but to me and Gypsy, "ranch" meant the house and barn and corrals and food and water and being in out of the snow.

I untied Gypsy and started to lead her up the side of the gully. She balked, but at last she gave it up, and we started out again, me on foot and her limping along behind me like she was going to drop dead any minute. Gypsy was cranky and didn't want to move, but I figured she didn't feel much worse than I did. Now I had to face the fact that the horses were somewhere in this far end of the big pasture—that's if they hadn't knocked this fence down, too, and taken off into the mountains—and without a horse to ride, I was going to have one rotten time leading them. Not to mention the fact that if I did find them there was no way on earth I could herd them into the partly fenced corral around the last spring. I had about as much chance of doing that as Pa would have of harnessing a wild bull to his plow. . . .

Harnessing a wild bull.

Harnessing.

Or—*roping.*

All at once I stopped. I stood there like a rock and stared at the sagebrush and the timber and the rimrocks fifty feet ahead of me, and I knew how I could do it. I knew how I could get lead ropes on Pet and Snip, and get them home.

There's not much bunchgrass in this end of the pasture, and the horses had already eaten a lot of it. But here and there I could find small clumps in heavy sage thickets, up against rocks, hidden away along tiny washes in the rimrocks where spring rains had left extra moisture. Bunch-grass is so valuable that anybody who lives out here just naturally gets used to seeing it, finding it, watching for it, memorizing where you'll find it. When I die and go to heaven, the only good deed I'll be able to tell St. Peter will be that I never destroyed any bunchgrass. And even if it doesn't help me with St. Peter, it'll go a long way with Pa....

And I had another thing going for me right now. Horses are grazers. They have a natural urge to keep moving as they feed, and that way they never really clean the grass out right down to the roots the way, for example, sheep do. I knew I could find grass here that they had missed.

I found a clump of pine trees and tied Gypsy where she would have some shelter. After I unsaddled her I put the saddle over a rock, untied the saddlebags, and hung them on a low tree branch. I stood the rifle scabbard against a rock out of the way of Gypsy's feet so she couldn't kick it over and get dirt in it, and also took the coils of rope and laid them aside. For a minute I thought about leaving the rifle here—I knew it would be hard to carry—but then I thought better of it. If nothing else, it would make me feel safer. I slid it out of the scabbard and, after thinking for a moment, I took one shell out of the box in my pocket and loaded it. Then, with the rifle in one hand, safety on, and the ropes in the other, I started out.

Twenty feet away I began to find grass. The clumps were small and hidden, but they were there. The snow was still only a couple of inches deep, and didn't hide the bunchgrass, which usually grows to ten or twelve inches tall. Down this close to the ground I could smell the sage as the falling snow made the tiny gray leaves damp. There was a faint damp smell from the ground, too, and I always liked that smell. Living on a near desert gives you a reason to like the smell of water anywhere you find it. I could have been just as happy smelling the dampness, though, if I'd been standing in a nice warm barn right now.

I worked for probably close to an hour. It was slow, but by then I had accumulated about two good-sized, packed-down arm-loads of dry grass, and I finally coaxed it all into a pile and wrapped several turns of one of the rope around it so I could carry the slippery stuff without spilling most of it.

By this time I was probably half a mile from Gypsy, and I sat down on a rock to rest for a minute and decide what to do. I didn't see any reason to go back to where I had Gypsy tied. She was safe and protected where she was, and I needed to save all the time I could. Now that I had some "bait" the next thing to do was locate the horses. And I could do that a lot better if I wasn't dragging her along behind me.

I was gambling on their still being here in the big pasture. If Rosie had knocked this fence down, too, then they would be loose out there on unfenced range, and there would be no way on earth I could bring them in. For that matter, by the time I could get home and tell Pa they were out, there'd be very little chance that the two of us could ever catch any or all of them, even if we got help from other ranchers. I've heard of horses that got out into the mountains before and either turned wild or just died from trying to survive without enough food or shelter. But somehow I had a feeling now that the horses were still here inside the big pasture. The main thing that convinced me was the fact that their signs—tracks and manure—here were fresh. If I could move fast enough and not make too many mistakes, I figured I still had a chance to bring at least some of them home.

I hoisted the bundle of grass onto my back and stood there for a second looking around. Three little knobby crests were ahead, all topped with rimrocks, and beyond that were more of the same. For a second I wondered if I'd made a mistake taking time to cut the grass instead of tracking the horses. But the fact was, the horses were now somewhere in an area probably no more than a mile or two square, and if you subtracted the tops of the rimrocks where they couldn't go, I really only had half that much ground to cover. And since I was no longer on horse-back, I probably had a much better chance of sneaking up on them before they saw me. Most of the sage here was as tall as I was, and I could take extra care whenever I had to cross an open space with no cover. Being on foot meant I couldn't see very far, but it also meant the horses couldn't see me, not to mention the fact that since Gypsy wasn't here with me, she wouldn't catch sight of the other horses and let out a whinny. One of the few things you can count on with horses is that when one horse comes up to another, he's going to whinny, whether you want him to or not. I figured I was about even, between the pluses and minuses.

I started up between the first two rim-rocks, keeping quiet, holding my head down. I saw some fresh manure and the tracks of a couple of horses, but nothing more. I circled the first low crest and started up between the next two, behind a rise from Gypsy and well hidden from any spooky horse that might be swinging his head up to look around. My whole plan—what there was of it—depended on sneaking up to the horses without Rosie or

Socks or Damfool seeing me. Any of them would spook and set the whole herd off at a dead run. What I had to do was slide up through the sage and get close enough to Pet or Snip to let them see the grass I was carrying. I knew they had to be hungry, feeding out here without barn hay and grain to fill them up, and besides, there isn't a horse alive that can resist bunchgrass.

For that matter, neither can any other grass-eater. Pa told me that when he was a little kid there used to be great herds of pronghorn antelope out here, and elk in the mountains. I wish I could have seen it then. Maybe the country would have looked different to me. All I can see now are great stretches of dry land, sage, and clumps of dark green mountains scattered here and there. The ranches are fenced now, and most of the pronghorn are gone; the bunchgrass that's left goes to feed workhorses and beef cattle. The first white men to come here were looking for gold, but what they found was bunchgrass. I guess bunchgrass is the closest thing to gold I'll ever see. . . .

Then, far ahead in a shallow draw with thick clumps of lodgepole pines, I heard a faint sound, and I came back to here and now in a heartbeat. Through the falling snow, the sound I heard was like a *click!*— soft, muted by distance, but I knew what it was. Somewhere up ahead of me an iron horseshoe had just struck against a rock.

I stooped down till I was almost bent double. I couldn't let a scrap of me show through the brush. I was silent—I didn't snap a twig or scrape my boot on a rock. I hardly breathed.

And then—I saw her. A bay mare, standing head down and rump into the wind as the snow riffled through her black tail. It was Pet. She had found a little shelter next to a cluster of big rocks, and she was facing away from me. Her colt stood by her head, but also facing away from me and away from the wind. His little tail flashed back and forth as he tried to brush away the snow as if it were a cloud of flies.

I squatted down behind a clump of brush, trying to take in everything as fast

as I could. I had to be careful. *Careful,*
God—I prayed—don't let me mess this
up. I'm only going to get one chance to do
this.

I thought fast. How could I come up
on Pet without her or the colt seeing me?
Pet is pretty gentle, but the colt, already
restless from cold and hunger, would
panic and run, and Pet would have to follow to guard her colt. Somehow I had to
make sure Pet saw the grass before she or
the colt got scared and started to run.

The rocks Pet had sheltered by were
big chunks of lava fallen from the rimrock
above her. The boulders overtopped the
two horses by three or four feet, and I
didn't think Pet was likely to be watching
for anything to come at her from up there.
If I could get up on the rocks—and push a
little of the grass over the edge—it would
fall practically at Pet's feet. And once Pet
saw bunchgrass falling out of the sky, she
would grab for it even if the devil himself
came out of the brush at her.

Slowly and carefully I slid through the
brush and around the back side of the

rocks. I leaned the rifle against the base of the rocks and climbed up onto them, taking care that my leather boots didn't slide on the hard rock surface. Silently I worked my elbows over the highest ledge and pulled myself up. For a second I lay flat. Then I pulled a dozen handfuls of grass out of the bundle, and pushed them off over the edge of the rock. I heard Pet snort in surprise, but I didn't hear her hooves pounding away in fright. I pushed more hay over—enough so she couldn't eat it all at once. Then I turned and slid down off the rocks. So far, so good.

I didn't have much time. There wasn't enough grass to last very long, and Pet would be hungry and would eat it fast. My feet hit the ground, and I took three long strides around the rocks. In a second I was at Pet's tail, her side, her head—

And then I had the rope around her neck, and tied in a bowline.

Pet's head came up like the boom on a crane. She banged her long, bony nose into the side of my head, and I felt like somebody had clouted me with a two-by-four. Then her hooves began to dance, and her big barrel swayed back and forth. But I held on as the blow made bright colors sparkle before my eyes, and a thudding sound echoed inside my head.

When my eyes cleared and I could see again, Pet's head was down, and she was shoveling in more grass. My rope was firm around her neck. I had her.

eleven

FOR A MINUTE I JUST STOOD THERE. I WAS PANTING as if I'd run a long way, even though I hadn't. I was so happy to have a rope on Pet, it was all I could do to keep from letting out a yell, right out there in the sagebrush and the snow. Even with a bruise throbbing on the side of my head, I was ready to celebrate.

But instead of yelling I quickly slid around behind Pet. If the rest of the horses were nearby, and I knew they had to be, they couldn't see me back here, except for my legs. And horses don't count worth anything—they don't seem to notice an extra pair of legs on the other side of a horse as long as they don't see the rest of you.

The colt had seen me, of course, and

had snorted and snapped up his head and jumped back, but I didn't hear anything that told me the other horses had taken alarm from the colt. Colts spook easy, and older horses learn to ignore it. The colt was dancing around fifteen feet away, his eyes rolling, but as he saw that his mother wasn't getting excited, he began to calm down. As he swung around I saw what I had already suspected: He was the one with the bloody wound. If a cougar had tried to attack the herd, he would be most likely to try to bring the colt down rather than a full-grown horse that could either put up some fight, or at least run away. There was a jagged tear in the colt's black hide from about the middle of his barrel almost to the flank. I hoped it wasn't too deep—the blood had clotted and dried by now, so it was hard to tell at this distance how bad it was.

Then, standing behind Pet, I leaned out just enough so I could see if the other horses were anywhere near. Yes. Over there was a rump, here a patch of shoulder, a tail, an ear—just glimpses through the brush told me they were within maybe fifty to a hundred feet, scattered in the tall brush and half-hidden among the trees. That looked like Socks there, the closest one, and the next one I was fairly sure of was Damfool—both of them restless, snorty animals that are hard enough to catch in a corral. Pa uses Socks as a saddle horse, but he is the only one who can ride him. There was no way I could hope to get a rope on either Socks or Damfool out here, and I wouldn't waste time trying.

The horse I had to find, before any of them found me, was Snip. Snip is a huge, gentle black mare and as she is Pet's daughter and has lived and worked next to Pet all her life, she wouldn't be far away now. And once I found her and got a rope on her, I would have no trouble getting her to follow Pet. And once I got leads on Pet and Snip and started for home, it was a fairly good bet that some of the others would follow. Maybe all of them. At least all of them except Ol' Rosie, and I didn't care whether she followed or not. Like Pa said, Ol' Rosie had probably cost us more in lost time and broken harness than she had ever earned. And as of now, she had cost me the best part of two days out here in the cold, and a lame horse, and God only knew what else could happen before I got any horses home for Pa.

But once I got ropes on both Pet and Snip, the worst that could happen would be that none of the other horses would follow me home. And even if that happened, I could still take Pet and Snip and Gypsy and the colt home, and we'd have them—though maybe not Gypsy—to use to come back for the others. Both Pet and Snip could be ridden bareback, and although they're slow, heavy workhorses, slow and heavy is better than nothing at all. And if it finally came to that, Pa could harness Pet and Snip to the wagon and go for help—get some ranchers who have good riding stock to help us round up ours. But that would be the very last thing Pa would do. Not that they wouldn't help—Pa would do the same, if someone needed him—but you don't load your problems on someone else's shoulders unless you absolutely have to.

By now I could see that Snip had to be a little farther out in the brush. I looked around and picked out a stout pine tree a few feet away, and then gathered up the grass I had given to Pet and, leading her partly with the rope and partly with the grass, I got her over to the tree without the rest of the horses seeing me. The colt was still tap-dancing around, but he stayed within a few feet of Pet, and I didn't think he would leave her.

I tied Pet up close and left her enough grass to keep her happy and, with the other rope in my hand, I started to make a wide circle around the horses to see if I could locate Snip. I carried the rest of the grass with me, but left the rifle where it was for now. I didn't want to accidentaly bump it against a rock and knock the safety off, or fall over my feet and jerk the trigger. If I spooked the horses now, I wouldn't see them again till kingdom come, and maybe not then.

The horses were scattered up the side of a fairly steep slope and in heavy cover that worked both for and against me. I couldn't see very far in any direction, but then neither could they, and with the snow still falling, they might not be so alert to anything moving. I slid from one clump of brush to another, trying not to rattle any dry twigs or stumble over a rock. I passed within fifteen feet of Prince, and saw Dandy just a little farther downslope from him, but there wasn't the slightest chance of getting a rope on them either—they are Pa's youngest horses, only three or four years old, and we still consider them only green-broke. They are the most likely of all the horses—except maybe Ol' Rosie herself—to bolt and run.

I slid quietly past Prince and Dandy, circling now a little downhill. The snow seemed to be falling heavier, and it was getting harder to see all the time. Falling snow makes movement everywhere, and it's hard to pick out a tail or an ear flicking.

And finally, when I was just about a full half-circle around from where I'd found Pet, I saw Snip. She was standing, head down, in the lee of a short, bushy pine tree where she had found a single little patch of dry grass. But there wasn't a rock or a tall bush nearby where I could slide up close to her.

I squatted down on my heels and tried to think of a way to get up close enough to her to get my rope around her neck before she could take off. Snip is tame and gentle, but not quite as tame and gentle as Pet, and she was going to be harder to catch. I still had a good bundle of grass, though, and I knew she would grab for it if she saw it. I had to figure out how to get it to her without scaring her off.

Or—how to get *her* to the grass. What if I just dropped it on the ground here, and then took a long branch and pushed the pile of grass out from behind the clump of bushes so that it would be where she could see it? Would she wonder how it got there? I didn't think so. I figured she'd eat first and ask questions later. And by that time I'd have my rope around her neck.

It worked.

I piled all the rest of my grass at the foot of a bush as close as I could get to Snip without her seeing me, picked up a long, twiggy branch of dead sagebrush and, using it like a hay fork, I carefully inched the bundle of grass out to where Snip could see it. She must have been dozing on her feet, because for a few seconds she didn't move. Then it was time for her to switch her weight from one hind leg to the other, the way they do when they're resting, and as she shifted she must have opened her eyes and looked around.

Her head jerked around, and her neck stretched out as she saw and scented the grass. A second later she was over to it and eating. And one second after that I had moved quietly around behind her, slipped my rope around her neck, and had the knot tied.

And I was standing there with my fingers still around the knot in the rope, feeling smart and telling myself that Pa would be proud of me—when all hell broke loose.

A scream like nothing I ever heard before ripped through the air.

Snip's head went up. She reared back on her hind legs—yanked me up in the air with her—and then slammed back down and took off straight up the side of the ridge. Dragging me with her—

Brush slapped and tore me—rocks

bruised me—I saw a pine tree coming at me—my feet went out from under me, and I fell facedown—

—But I held on to the rope.

And she stopped.

I lay there on the ground with my face in the snow. Pain stabbed through me—my knees—my shoulder—my face—

Then I heard something heavy drumming on the ground near my head. I knew it was Snip's hooves, and if she came down on me there on the ground I would never get up again. Sweating, dizzy, sick with pain, I rolled over and climbed to my feet. I didn't even open my eyes. I was afraid to. But I held on to the rope.

I stood there as if I'd been blindfolded, shaking and weak, for half a minute, maybe more. I got to open my eyes, I thought.

I could hear Snip snorting, her breath whistling. She was still jerking her head to look all around. If I had let go or even slacked my hold for a second, she would have been gone again. The cougar—I knew it was a cougar that had screamed—must have made a strike and missed. But he would still be out there. And I knew that all the other horses except Pet and Gypsy who were tied up would have run off God knows where into the brush.

I got my left eye open. Looked around.

There was a big black shape in front of me. That was Snip. Trees all around. Rock beside me, and in front of me. That was what had stopped Snip. She hadn't been able squeeze past the rocks with me dragging along beside her like an anchor.

I took a deep breath. My knees hurt— probably skinned. My right shoulder hurt— sprained from holding on to the rope. My head hurt. Couldn't see too good.

Finally I realized that my right eye was still shut. I reached up to feel of it. There was a slimy flap of skin hanging down over it and under that a mound of torn-up flesh. I knew the slime was blood. I gritted my teeth and pushed my fingers into the mess, forced the eyelid open.

I could still see.

Shaking, I let the eyelid close again.

I stood there for another minute, trying to think. The wind had been knocked out of me, but I was beginning to breathe better now, and I wasn't quite so dizzy. I had a confused feeling that, as bad as things were, there was something good here, too, if I could just figure out what it was.

For the second time I made a list of bad things in my mind: Snow. I was miles from home. It was late afternoon—soon be dark. I was hurt—bleeding. Gypsy was lame. Worst of all, I knew that the cougar was out there—close to me and he was hunting. I still had the rifle, but it was only a .22. A rifle that light isn't big enough to stop a cougar. It would kill a rattlesnake, or a rabbit to eat, but even if I got off a shot that hit the cougar, it wouldn't bring it down. I couldn't depend on it to save me. It was a damn long list of bad things.

Then I tried to think of what the good thing might be. And finally it came to me: I had done what I'd come to do. I had roped Pet. I had roped Snip.

I tightened my grip on the rope and turned to lead Snip back to where Pet was tied.

All I had to do now was go home.

twelve

THE HORSES, ALL EXCEPT THE THREE I HAD ROPES on and the colt, were scattered from hell to breakfast, but I didn't care. There was nothing more I could do here. I was sore and bloody, and it was going to be even harder to see now with only one good eye. The only thing left for me was to take what I had and head for the ranch, and hope to God I could get there before it got too dark and the snowfall too heavy for me to travel, or before the cougar hit again.

As I stumbled along with Snip's hooves thudding heavily behind me, I watched the weather. The snowfall had stayed about the same all day. It was very cold, so the flakes stayed small, but they were falling with that peculiar spiraling motion that looked as if the storm would last forever. Under the heavy clouds it would be full dark earlier than usual, and I had no lantern. What I did have was a pounding pain behind my right eye, which had swelled shut and was now sealed in a mass of torn skin and clotted blood.

It took ten minutes or more to get back to where Pet was tied. I kept stumbling over rocks and into sagebrush. Once, I fell clear to my knees, but Snip threw her head up to look around and she pulled me up with her.

I lost my directions once but finally I caught sight of the tree where Pet was tied. She had torn up the ground and probably stretched her rope to the breaking point when she heard the cougar scream, but she was there and she was safe. The colt was there, too, huddled close to her side.

When Pet saw Snip she let out a big whinny, and Snip answered her, and then the colt chimed in. All three of them had to sniff each other's muzzles and stamp their hooves a few times and cough—I guess they were telling each other how they felt about things like snow and ropes and cougars. They probably had a few things to say about me, too. I wished I had somebody to talk to, too, but I was in a hurry to get moving. I tied Snip up for a minute and went around the rocks to get my rifle. Light as it was, it was better than no gun at all. I knew I had to get back to Gypsy soon, because that cougar was still out there somewhere and I didn't know if he had scented her and attacked. If the cougar went for her, she wouldn't be able to put up much of a fight.

The rifle was where I had left it, and I picked it up and brushed the snow off. Then I went back and untied Pet and Snip and wound their leads around my left hand and, with the rifle in my right hand— safety off this time—I started back to where I had left Gypsy. The colt, after some false starts off into the brush, turned and followed as Pet whinnied a couple of sharp blasts into his ear. The colt was nervous, and limping a little, too. I hoped the blood on his wound had dried. The cougar was twice as likely to strike again if he scented blood, and instinct would tell him he had wounded the colt and now it would be easier to bring him down.

Gypsy was where I had left her tied to the pine tree, but I could tell from the way she had torn up the ground that she had heard the cougar and done her best to break loose. She was snorty and spooky and even with her lame leg she managed to bang into me a couple of times while I was tying Pet and Snip up beside her.

Then, with the three horses safe, I sat down on a rock and took a couple of minutes to think. There was this much about it—by finally coming up on the horses at this far east end of the big pasture, we were only a mile or so from a wire gate that leads into a smaller cow pasture that lies up the slope from the barn. And the small pasture itself isn't much more than a couple of miles square, and fairly open and grassy. I didn't have to backtrack all the way I had come yesterday and today: it was a simple matter of finding the wire gate— and it would be hard to locate in the dark—

and then leading the horses through it and on down to the barn. For all of yesterday and today I had been traveling roughly in a big circle, but the arc of the circle I was on now put me and the horses much closer to home than I would have been yesterday, if I had found them sooner. All I had to do now was just get started and keep moving, with no more stops or slowdowns on the way.

But the first thing to do was eat. I went to the saddlebags and took out three biscuits and what was left of the ham. By eating now I wouldn't even have to stop long enough to get the food out of the saddlebags.

As I ate, I tried to figure out how much daylight I had left. I knew there wasn't much. An hour of fair light, and maybe a half hour of fading light, and finally darkness. And as the night comes on, you can easily lose all sense of direction, especially when snow is falling. I would have to guide myself mostly by the slope under my feet. As long as I was going downhill, I would be going more or less in the right direction.

It was the time that worried me the most. Depending on how fast Gypsy could travel, it would take easily three or four hours to make it home. I would have to stop every half mile or so and let Gypsy rest. I could walk and lead the horses as long as I could see fairly well through the falling snow. But once it got full dark, I would have to fall back on an old cowhand's trick that Pa taught me: When you are lost, or it's too dark to see, give your horse his head, and he will take you home. When that time came, I would link the three horses together on short ropes, with Pet in the lead. Then I would take a running jump and get up on her, and then I would simply give her a loose rein, and Pet would take us home. She would find her way down off the high ridge where we were now, through the trees and tangled gullies and rimrocks and lower ridges that dropped down to the long slope of the basin where the ranch house was. She would find the gate that led from the big pasture into the small cow pasture that we had to cross, even when I couldn't see it myself. Now that Pet and the other horses were roped and back in the control of a person (I prayed), something in their minds would start to work like this: Barn. Hay. Oats. Warm. No cougar. Good. Let's go—

Yes, Pet would get us home, even if I couldn't.

When I had finished eating I stowed the empty towels in the saddlebags. I put the saddle on Gypsy and cinched it down tight even though I didn't plan to ride her. I tied the saddlebags on and the rifle scabbard, and finally tried to think of the best way to line the horses up for now. If Gypsy was in the lead she would hold the others back, but if she was last in line the other two would pull her along and set a better pace. So I tied Snip to follow Pet, and Gypsy so she would follow Snip. The colt would tag along somewhere near his mother. I double-checked my knots to make sure none of them opened up. Then I picked up Pet's lead in my left hand and the rifle in my right. For one more second I stood there. If Ma was here she would tell me to pray now, I thought, but I'm in a hurry.

Then I remembered the cougar.

"God'lmighty, help me get home. In Jesus' name. Amen."

Then I turned and started down the hill.

For a while walking wasn't too bad. I could still see brush and rocks and steep patches where I might slide. I was leading Pet on a short rope and I didn't want to fall in front of her—I knew she probably wouldn't step on me if she could help it, but there was no sense in taking chances. The descent was steep, and all I could see was the cloud of whirling snowflakes; I felt like the little tin man in one of those glass globes that are filled with water and when you shake the globe the snow flies all around inside. But of course the little tin man isn't real, and I am. And I am cold. Cold. Cold.

I tried to fight the cold by thinking of warm blankets and sitting by the cookstove at night, watching the orange fire dancing in the firebox. Hot coffee—hot stew—hot biscuits—

I wished I could say to Pet, "Hey, I'm hungry. I'm tired. I'm cold. Can't you walk a little faster?" And she would say—

Well, I guess Pet wouldn't say anything. No matter how much I talked to her, Pet would never answer me. Too bad. I could use a little cheerful conversation right now. And all at once I remembered the time Davy tried to get me to make Trixie, the dog, talk to him. . . .

I guess he must have been lonesome with Ma and Pa, even me, mostly too busy to pay any attention to him. He probably started talking to the dog, and now he had gotten to wondering why the dog wouldn't talk to him. He was only about three years old then, and it must have seemed to him that Trixie could talk, if she just would.

He is always with Trixie—there isn't much time in the day when he isn't. Sometimes they are playing, and sometimes not doing anything special. Just together. If Ma gives him a bowl of mush for breakfast or beans for lunch, he'll carry it outside and sit on the back stoop and eat it with Trixie lying there at his feet, waiting for a bite. And he always saves the last little bit for her. Ma used to say that when Davy learned to walk she always knew where he was because she'd look for Trixie, and Davy would be there, too. They play hide-and-seek, and run races. They even take naps together. I guess that's why Davy sometimes gets to smelling kind of like a dog, too.

So I shouldn't have been surprised that day when he came out to the pigpen where I was throwing grain into the trough and said, "Wart—how come Trixie don't talk to me?"

I thought he was kidding. Didn't answer.

"Wart, how come?"

I was trying to spread the grain in the long, V-shaped trough so that all the pigs could eat, but the biggest sow, Red, had straddled the trough, and none of the others could get any feed. I took up a big, heavy stick that we kept by the pen for times like these and poked her in the side. But even when I scraped the sharp point of the stick up and down her dirty red skin, she just went on eating.

"Wart, how come?" Davy's dark eyes

were real serious. In his little bib overalls he looked like some kind of talking doll himself.

I leaned out and whacked Red over the back, but she didn't move. She had her huge head down, and her alligator-sized jaws were scooping up grain like she planned to eat it all. I was supposed to see to it that all the pigs got a fair share. It's real hard to explain to a pig about fair shares. I brought the stick down over her head, but she just flapped her ears like dirty red flags and went on shoveling in the grain. The younger sows were squealing and snapping their teeth at her. Any minute now one of them would draw blood, and then a nice fight would break out. It was summer, and wounds would be flyblown and crawling with maggots inside of two days. "I need a pitchfork," I grunted. I was hanging half over the heavy timber fence around the pigpen so I could bang at the sow, and the hot stink of pig came up like a cloud in my face. I was beginning to feel like throwing up.

"*How come*, Wart?" Davy was tugging on my shirt, like he thought I really had the answer here.

"Jeez-uz—" I hollered. "How do *I* know? Ask Trixie—"

"I did. She don't *say* nothing, Wart. *You* tell her to talk to me."

I was beginning to boil. It only takes a little pig stink to set me off. And with Davy nagging me about why the *dog* doesn't *talk*—"Dammit, Davy, if I could talk to a dog, I could talk to a pig—and I'd tell that ol' sow to git outta the trough before I brain her—" I grabbed up Pa's pitchfork that was leaning against the fence and raised it like a spear.

Davy screamed. "Don't jab her, Wart! You'll hurt her—"

"That's what I mean to do!"

Davy scrambled up onto the fence. "Move, Red!" he hollered. "Move over! Hurry up or Wart'll pitchfork you!"

The huge sow raised her head—a head that was as big as Davy's whole body—and looked at him. Her mouth gaping open showed razor-sharp teeth two inches long that could easily bite through a man's arm. Her little eyes glittered.

"Move over!" cried Davy again, waving his hand inches from the powerful jaws and sharp fangs. Then he tapped her lightly on the side of her neck.

Instantly the sow shifted her huge two-clawed feet and daintily swung her two-hundred-pound rump around. Seconds later she was lined up with all the other sows, politely swilling down her share of the grain.

I put the pitchfork down. "Don't— don't tell Pa I almost pitchforked the sow," I whispered.

"Okay. But you gotta make Trixie talk to me."

And I . . . promised to try.

Now, out here in the snow, I sure wished I had been able to persuade Trixie to talk to Davy. At least it would have been something to remember that I'd managed to do right.

It took half an hour to work down off the high ridge. Gypsy was laying back and

dragging on her rope so bad that sometimes Pet and Snip just stopped. I let
Gypsy rest a few minutes every so often,
and then I had to holler and yell and yank
on Pet's lead and get them all started again.
Pet and Snip were no problem, except that
Pet kept looking around to make sure her
colt was close by. The colt was limping, too,
of course, and by now he was tired and
hungry, and he kept falling back. I couldn't
go back after him—he would just run from
me—so I had to gamble on his following.

When we got down the last steep pitch
of the ridge we would have to work our
way through a patch of heavy juniper forest. In dry country or high desert, junipers
grow very scattered, but where there is
a spring or a natural basin that catches
runoff, they grow closer, and this place
was maybe a couple of acres square where
the sloping side of a very open gully had
funneled water down off nearby ridges.
There were big outcrops of rocks here also,
and one place where the leading edge of
an old lava flow ended, leaving a ten-foot-
high rimrock. I didn't look forward to going

through the trees, but it would take too long to try to drag my tired, limping train of horses around them.

All at once I heard a noise. Something I couldn't quite identify—over and above the padded fall of my horses' hooves, the creak of leather from the saddle. I listened, holding my breath. Yes—there it was again. A sliding, scuffling sound. Faint, muffled thudding. A snort. A cough.

Turning very slowly, very carefully, I looked back. There—dark shape—another. Dark shapes crusted with snow—snow on their backs, snow on their ears, down the long sloping faces and muzzles, even on the tufts of short hair at the base of their tails. They were so coated with white that they looked like horses made of snow. And I knew that the other horses—or some of them— were following me home to the barn!

No—I corrected that right away. They were doing what Pa had said they might do—and I had hoped they would: They were following Pet. After letting crazy Ol' Rosie lead them up here into the wilds where there was no manger full of nice oat hay and no grain in the feed box, no warm barn, not even a good drink of water, they'd had enough of freedom, and now it was time to follow dependable old Pet back toward the place where they knew there would be hay and oats, and a nice, warm barn where they would be out of the snow.

I leaned my head against Pet and almost bawled. It had worked—the one thing we couldn't plan on, but hoped for—it had worked. Now, with just a little more dumb luck, I might be able to get them through the gate and down to the barn without anything else going wrong. Pa, I knew, would have put out fresh hay in the corral and in the mangers in the barn, hoping that if I got them back—when I got them back—and they got close enough, they would smell it and come on in.

Maybe there was a chance this day would end right yet.

Thirteen

I COULDN'T SEE MUCH AS WE ZIGZAGGED DOWN through the brush on the lower slope, but I began to feel that something was different. My feet were sliding in the snow, and my hat and shoulders were piled with it, but it began to seem as if it wasn't coming down as heavily as it had been. I jerked quick looks off to the left and right and I was almost sure that the moving cloud of white was thinning. A little more hope began to build inside me. If only it would stop snowing, the rest of the trip home wouldn't be half so hard. I would still be hurting and half-blind, tired and cold, and Gypsy lame, but at least we would be able to see better, even after full dark.

Because there is this funny thing about snow. After the snow has stopped falling and the ground is covered, there is light. I don't know why, but it's true. You can walk all around on a dark night with snow on the ground, and you can see. The falling snow cuts off all vision, but when it stops, and the snow is on the ground, it's as if the snow has light in it. It's as if light comes up from the ground.

I remembered a night last winter when we had had a heavy snowfall all day, and when it stopped Pa had to go out and look for a young heifer that had wandered off somewhere. She was a real dumb animal— always the one to stick her head through a barbwire fence and get cut, or step on a gopher snake and then go crazy and run for half a mile. Pa decided not to take any of the saddle horses because horses don't go that good in deep snow, and he was pretty sure the heifer wasn't too far off. For some reason he called me to go with him, and I'm glad he did. I learned about snow that night.

We put on heavy boots and coats and

tied our hats down with mufflers over our ears, and Pa took a short length of rope, not to lead the heifer but to snap over her head like a whip. Pa never actually whips any of our animals, but sometimes he says you have to make them think you will, just to get it across to them that you are the boss. So then we started out over the rolling cow pasture where the cows had been earlier, and it was like we were walking through drifted moonlight. The sky was clear and full of ice-colored stars—there was no moon—and the snow on the ground seemed almost to glow. Every tree stood out like an ink-black drawing, and even dry stalks of weeds and grass were outlined against the white. I couldn't see any color at all—I knew Pa's coat was a red plaid mackinaw, and mine was a brown plaid, but they were just shades of gray now. Our faces were pale like the inside of a shell, and Pa's hat and jeans and boots were dark as sable. He walked a little in the lead, breaking trail for me, and I watched his boots as they sank into the snow with every step.

There were coyotes out hunting that night, and we heard them howling from all sides. To the east, toward Boulder Creek, we heard one, and to the south, toward the high hills where I was now, there were two, and to the north and west, down across the open basin, there must have been half a dozen more. Their voices are high-pitched, like sopranos, but instead of words to music they sing a few short notes and then follow with a long, long, drawn-out descending sprinkle of tones that softens away into silence. Then they start the song all over again. It was like we were walking through music instead of air.

We found the heifer and brought her back to the barn, and I don't remember much about coming home, but I will never forget walking with Pa through that glowing light, with the sound of coyote music echoing mile after mile around us.

fourteen

About the same time that I realized it was no longer snowing, I also realized that we were almost to the trees. There was a short slope ahead of us now as we came down off the flank of the ridge, and the sagebrush here was short and stunted. But ahead, in the swale, rose the outer fringe of the juniper forest, and here the sage was tall, with heavy, splintery stems and twigs that were strong enough to scratch and draw blood if you found yourself plowing through them.

I got to ride, I thought. At least to the other side of the trees. Paying out slack on my rope, I worked my way back to Gypsy and slid the rifle into the scabbard on the saddle. I knew I couldn't hold it and get up onto Pet, and right now all I wanted to do was keep moving, as fast as possible. I pulled on the rope, and Pet slowed a little, finally stopped. Holding the rope in my right hand, I stood just behind her right shoulder, bounced a couple of times, and tried to bounce high enough to throw my head, shoulders, and belly up onto her back. Tried twice, fell back twice. Each time I missed, Pet eased slowly forward a step or two. Finally she just took off walking again, with me dragging along beside her. I hauled her up again, tried the jump again. It wasn't that hard or that high— I'd done it hundreds of times before. But now I was tired and cold, half-sick with the pounding I'd taken, and it felt like I was trying to jump up onto the roof of a house. I tried again, fell back again. Pet oozed forward, Snip and Gypsy shuffling after her.

Dammit. I'd spent two days trying to round these rotten horses up to get them back to the ranch, and now that I'd got them moving and pointed in the right direction, I couldn't get them stopped. Pet had got it into her head that she was going to the barn, and she didn't want to hear anything different now.

I lumbered along beside her while some good, strong cuss words rattled around in my head.

I thought about trying to lay the rope up over her back like reins, then back off ten feet or so and take a running jump at her—I could probably get up enough speed that way to push myself up onto her back. Trouble was—I could see that the minute I let the rope out of my hand, Pet would just take off again. Pet, Snip, Gypsy, the colt, and whatever number of the other horses that were behind us were wound up and headed for home, and they were just hungry and cold enough to keep on going till they got there. It reminded me of those jokes I'd heard about the new automobiles. You got them started, and then they just kept on going, no matter how loud you hollered, "Whoa!" But of course if a person had an automobile, he'd be rich to start with and he wouldn't be out stumbling around in a pasture in the middle of the night in a snowstorm trying to round up horses. Or if he did have the horses, he'd send the hired man out. . . .

For a few more yards I plodded along beside Pet, still cussing, ready to bawl, when all at once I saw a squarish, blocky shape coming toward me. A rock. Pet would walk within inches of it, and it was only about two feet high.

Still holding the rope, I bounded forward and onto the rock a split second before Pet came abreast of it, turned, and flung myself onto her back.

Pet's head snapped up, and she snorted. I felt her gather her huge rear end together to punch a man-killing kick out behind her—but then she unwound. Decided it was too cold, too late, too something, to take offense at me on her back. Her head dropped back down, and she plunged forward into the trees.

At first it seemed very dark among the junipers, but that was just because there were so many humpy black shapes crowded close together here. Junipers are funny trees—they grow in all different patterns, no two alike, and they're often as wide as they are tall. They don't make a nice, dignified forest like pines, or a beautiful forest like spruce. They're not even friendly looking like firs. Junipers look like a lot of brothers and sisters in a big, ugly family, where they are all equally ugly but in different ways.

I was jolting along dodging branches, feeling Pet's big hooves hitting the ground, pa-*pum*, pa-*pum*, when all at once I looked up and saw, framed between Pet's ears, the edge of the rimrock. It was a narrow tongue of an old lava flow, and this finger-shaped ridge of rock ran down into the trees and then ended suddenly, as if the volcano had said, "Oh, the hell with it—that's enough," and stopped pouring out any more lava. The flow ended in a rounded bulge of rough black-red rock, and it was maybe ten feet high at the spot where Pet was going to pass less than an arm's length from it.

Damn.

All at once I stopped thinking about ugly junipers and started thinking about cougars again. That rimrock was tailor-made for a cougar to spring from—and if he did—

I yanked on the rope. Swung it hard to the left, away from the rimrock.

Pet plodded forward—the rimrock wasn't fifteen feet ahead of us.

I pulled on the rope. Left—to the left, dammit—

Thud, thud. Straight ahead. Then we were nearing—abreast of the rimrock—I looked up—

Nothing happened.

No scream. No huge cat launched itself out like a hungry devil coming down on us.

Pa-*pum*, pa-*pum*. Stride by stride, Pet went forward. The rimrock fell ten feet behind, fifteen, twenty. We were in the clear.

Feeling a wave of relief—the cougar must have given up on the horses and faded back into its own country, the high mountains—I felt a tight knot of fear deep inside me unwind. Now all I had to do was just stay where I was, feel the narrow ridge of Pet's spine like the top rail of a board fence between my legs, and the slide of my knees against her ribs. I had my left hand clamped on her mane where it fell down over her withers—just in case she stumbled, I wouldn't fall off—and with my right hand I kept a big slack in Pet's lead rope. She didn't need me to guide her now—she knew exactly where she was going, and nothing was going to stop her as she steered an easy course straight ahead through a small clearing in the trees. Snip at her heels was probably half-asleep, because all she had to do was follow Pet's tail a few inches in front of her nose. Gypsy was still limping but, like Snip, she would keep on going with the rope around her neck and Snip's tail bobbing along ahead of her. I wished I knew which horses, or how many, were following us back, but there was no way I could figure it out now. I glanced to my left just as the colt came dancing out from behind

Gypsy. He might have taken a blow, but he still had energy enough to toss his head and whisk his short little tail—

And then I saw it. A huge black blur exploded out of the trees to my left—a shape that ran—that sprang—

It hit the colt like a battering ram. The colt staggered.

I yelled. My rifle—oh, God—it's on the saddle—

I hit the ground—rope flung away—as I careened wildly back to Gypsy—ripped the rifle out of the scabbard.

Pet screamed and lunged toward her colt. The colt screamed. It crumpled under the black shape.

With the rifle I leaped forward. I couldn't see—if I shoot, I'll hit the colt—Pet—oh, God—

Then I heard something coming. A freight train—an avalanche—hooves pounding—neck stretched out—teeth showing in the snow-light—

It was Rosie—

She reared—reared—striking out with those hooves that were like war clubs—

The cougar rolled back, a squirming black shape against the snow. The colt fell away, staggered to its feet.

Rosie screamed and reared again— her front hooves stabbed out—

The cougar sprang at her.

But Rosie's strike came first. She came down on the cat with both hooves—I heard bones snap. The cat screamed and screamed, but he was on the ground, in the snow, and Rosie had a ton of bone and muscle to throw at a killer—

She reared again—I could smell blood—

And suddenly the black shape on the snow lay still.

Rosie reared again. And again. Then she backed slowly away. Her sides were heaving, and I knew there was red blood on her hooves. Even in the near darkness I could see her terrible shivering, the faint light shining on her wild eyes.

Suddenly Rosie wheeled around and screamed again, struck out with her right front hoof one more time at the body of the cougar. Her huge barrel bellowed out a cry, as if to say, "I killed it! I killed it!" For one more moment she was there, every muscle in her huge body tensed to kill more—to kill again. Then she spun around, snorting out the stink of blood and cat. And with a final strike at the cat, she plunged away, back up the slope through the trees and up toward the ridge, the way we had come. She was running full out—the thunder of her hooves drummed against the trees. I listened as if I'd been frozen there and would never move again.

At last the sound died away, and I could no longer hear it. Ol' Rosie was gone.

But I knew it didn't matter. I knew that nobody would ever try to catch Ol' Rosie again. Ol' Rosie had won. Ol' Rosie was finished. She had killed her devil, and she deserved to go free. . . .

fifteen

I DON'T KNOW HOW LONG I STOOD THERE, alone, in the clearing with the body of the cougar. I didn't go close and look at it; it was dead. I didn't want to see any more. I was shaking and sick to my stomach.

The rifle was still in my hand, and finally I reached over with my left hand and set the safety to "on." Pa would probably have told me to do that if he'd been here. Of course, Pa would probably have said a lot of other things, too, if he'd been here: "How come you weren't watching for the cougar? Why didn't you go *around* the trees? And where are the horses?—"

I snapped my head around. Oh, God.

The horses—Pet, Snip, Gypsy, the colt—they were gone.

I started to run, back toward the rim-rock and the ridge. And stopped. Wait a minute. I don't see any horses up this way. And Pet and Snip and Gypsy are still tied together. If they're still in the trees, they'll probably wind their rope up on a tree somehow. Turn around. Go back. Search the trees.

I found the three horses still roped together with the trailing lead that I had dropped caught in the dead snag of a tree split by lightning. They were scared and snorty and doing their best to yank themselves free; if I hadn't gotten there when I did, they would have snapped the rope just by throwing their weight against it. And then they would have taken off at a dead run.

"Ho, Pet. Ho, Snip. Ho, Gypsy." I started talking softly as I walked toward them. After all I'd been through, I didn't want to finish up with a horse kicking my ribs in when we were only a few miles from home. "Ho, Pet, ho, girl—"

Pet's ears flagged back and forth, and her big hooves were plowing furrows in the snow. She snorted and reared her head back, but then she reached out her muzzle to smell me. I could see she knew it was me—but she still raised a hind foot to kick me if she could, just to let me know how she felt about cougars and blood and screaming—

"Ho, Pet." I was still shaking but I was beside her now and, slowly and carefully, I reached up and laid my arms around her powerful neck. She is a gentle horse, but even a gentle horse is a horse. "Easy, girl. Easy, now. It's all right. Nothing to be afraid of now. It's all right. Easy, girl. Now let's go home—"

We had to get away from here as fast as we could. As long as the horses could still smell the dead cougar there was a danger they could bolt, and the rope that was holding them would snap like a piece of string if they really made up their minds to go—and all happened to pull in the same direction at once. Pa's always reminding me that a horse is bigger than you are, and stronger than you are, but you are smarter. Most of the time. Some of the time . . .

Moving quietly, I worked my way around to the other side of Pet. I shifted the rifle to my left hand and got my right hand on the lead rope where it was tied around Pet's neck. Then I started following the rope down to where it was clamped into the dead snag. I found it quickly and started to pull. It was like trying to pull something out of the jaws of a vise, with someone three times my size holding the vise shut. I pulled till my head throbbed and I thought my eye would start to bleed again. But then I happened to remember that the horses hadn't been able to pull it out by pulling straight ahead, so what made me think I could? Then I tried yanking upward on it, to see if I could work it out that way. Nothing worked.

I stood there and looked down at the rope, and I started to shake again. Was I going to fail now because a damn rope was caught and wouldn't come loose? I could feel anger boiling up in me. I wanted to scream and holler and cuss. I raised my right hand up high—if I had an ax right now, I'd chop that—ax?

I stood there and let my hand fall. Reached in under my coat to the pocket of my jeans, and took out my knife. . . .

From the trees down to the gate into the cow pasture was still a little over half a mile. Not far. On a summer day if I am feeling good I can run that far and hardly get short of breath. There is a pretty good trail along the bottom of the shallow gully if you keep your eye out for rocks and sagebrush roots. In the summer, when I used to run down the path, I had to watch out for rattlesnakes, but then you had to watch for rattlesnakes everywhere. . . .

Like the time two summers ago when Pa jumped down out of the hayloft in the barn into the center haymow half full of hay, and landed right on a big diamond-back. The snake was hunting mice, I guess, and he didn't like it when Pa came down on top of him. He bit Pa on the leg—his fangs went in just above the top of Pa's boot. Pa killed the snake with his pitch-fork—ran the tines through him till he got the head—and then he staggered to the house and told Ma what had happened. Ma pulled his pants and boot off and grabbed her butcher knife and made two crossed cuts where the fang marks were. Then she bent down—Pa was sprawled on the kitchen floor—and she sucked the blood and poison out. I'll always remember how Ma looked—sick and white and ready to throw up, but sucking out that blood. There was blood running down her chin onto her yellow dress. Davy and I stood there by the kitchen stove. Davy was cry-ing. I was so scared, I couldn't cry. So scared. I never saw my pa lie like that—it was like the world was coming to an end. I was screaming inside myself: "God—help him—help him—God, don't let him die—don't let him die—don't let him die—" Ma poured whiskey on the wound and band-aged it with strips torn from one of her sheets. Pa was awful sick for days. I went out to the barn and found the snake and I took it, still stuck on the tines of Pa's pitchfork, and threw it into the pigpen. Pigs are hell on snakes—they grabbed it and tore it apart. It was the meanest thing I could think of to do to a rattlesnake.

But there were no rattlesnakes out now. They'd be denned up somewhere down in gopher holes or deep inside the rock ledges, sleeping out the cold days, maybe dreaming about who they'd bite when summer came again. I kind of felt around inside me to find out if I had any anger, any hate, left for those rattlesnakes, but I didn't find any. A rattlesnake isn't something you have to hate; you just have to deal with it when you meet it on the trail. Inside me now was nothing much but a kind of empty place, with an outside shell of muscles that were still pushing me along on numb feet down a rocky slope, leading three horses and a colt some-where.

Somewhere. Yes, I was leading them, but . . . where? I tried to remember. *Where?* Oh—the gate. Yes—the gate. Up ahead was a gate, and I had to find it, open it, and go through. And lead my horses through it.

And something else . . . oh, yes. Close it. Close the gate. Pa gets real mad when somebody leaves a gate open when he ought to shut it. It seemed like a long, long time ago that somebody had left a gate open, and that had something to do with my being out here now. . . .

"I'm acting funny," I said. Pet heard me and swiveled her head around to look at me, so I knew I had said it out loud. "I'm acting real funny."

I thought about that for a while, and wondered why I was acting funny. I don't usually act funny. I better not act funny around Pa. Pa gets real mad when people act funny, crazy. Like the time Ma planted sweet peas and Pa said he thought they were weeds and hoed them up. Ma got so mad at him, she threw a whole pile of kitchen stove wood—hit him quite a few times, too. Pa wouldn't throw anything at her, or try to stop her—he said he'd never hit a woman and wasn't going to now—but he said she was crazy and he slept in the barn for two nights. But he brought her home three great big flowerpots of geraniums—rode all the way to Prineville just to get them. Next day he had to turn around and rode all the way back to take a bunch of calves to sell. I still remember how he looked driving up to the house in the old wagon with those three pots of geraniums on the open seat beside him. Ma let him back in the house when he gave her the geraniums, and she keeps growing more from the first ones, and she's got them in coffee cans all over the kitchen. Pa always claimed it was an accident he hoed up the sweet peas, but Pa knows the name of every plant he's ever seen, and I don't think Ma believed him. And whenever they have a fight now Ma picks up two or three cans of geraniums and sets them around close by her.

I was still thinking about the geraniums, and the little four-petaled flowers so red, they hurt your eyes, when all at once I realized I was standing still.

I looked around. Pet was pretty much just a big black shape a little ahead of me, and I could see she was standing still. Then

I reached out, and a few inches ahead of Pet's muzzle was a strand of barbwire. And in front of me, a little to her right, was a wooden pole, with a heavier post four or five inches to the right of it.

The gate. We had come to the gate.

While I was stumbling along thinking about rattlesnakes and geraniums, Pet had paced off the last mile, bringing Snip and dragging Gypsy after her, and now she was standing at the gate, waiting for me to open it.

Yeah. Got to open the gate. Been trying for two days to get some horses back to the gate, and through it. Got to open the gate. . . .

With fingers so numb with the cold that I could hardly feel anything, I tied my lead rope to the big post. Then I slid in between Pet and the gate and wrapped my left arm tight around the end pole of the gate and my right arm around the big, heavy post. Squeezed hard. Nothing moved.

Wire gates are hard to open. They're made with a little spring, almost a stretch, to them. You have to squeeze the gate pole up tight to the big post so you can slip the wire loop off the top of the gate. I clamped my arms as hard around the gate pole as I could. Pulled. Pulled. Finally, just as I felt my arms start to quiver and turn loose, I felt the loop start to slide up. I clenched my arms and then jabbed upward at the loop. There was a faint creaking sound, and the loop slipped up, and the gate pole sprang back, open. Just in time I lunged in front of Pet and kicked the gate out of the way so she and the other horses wouldn't walk through the tangled loops of barb-wire on the ground. Pet put her head down and snorted—maybe she knew the gate on the ground would be dangerous—and then I just had time to rip the knot out of her lead rope. In a second, Pet was plodding through the open gate, with the other horses at her heels.

Pet was a few feet past the gate when she lowered her head and snorted at some-thing on the ground. Cow manure. Now at last it was real—we were through the gate and into the cow pasture. If it had been daylight I could almost have seen the ridge-pole of the barn from where I was now. We were almost home.

Then something stopped me. I looked back at the gate. I knew it lay on the ground. I could hear Pa say, "Don't *never* leave a gate open. *Never.*" Pa would forgive a man for stealing or cheating before he'd excuse him for finding a gate shut and then leaving it open after he went through. When I get to heaven I'm going to have to be sure to close the Pearly Gate behind me when St. Peter lets me in.

I went back to the gate. Picked it up, put the bottom of the pole in the wire loop, and started trying to pull the pole up tight enough to get the top loop over it. Tried. Tried. Tried.

My arms started to shake again. I looked around. Pet was easing slowly onward toward the barn. I leaned my head against the gatepost. I wanted to go to the barn, too.

I felt my numb hands peel away from the pole and the post, and the wire gate crumpled at my feet. "I can't do it, Pa," I whispered. "I just . . . can't . . . do it . . ." I turned to follow the horses.

I walked maybe twenty yards in the dim light, watching the big black shape of the horses ahead of me and listening to the soft padding of their hooves on the snow-covered ground. And then I heard another faint noise behind me.

I turned. Snowy shapes were moving through the gate toward me. Horses. The other horses were still following. And all of us were going to the barn.

God, I'm so glad I didn't close that gate. . . .

sixteen

To the barn. After a long day of plowing or pulling a hay wagon or herding cattle or sheep, that's what a horse would want— probably even more than to be put out to pasture. He'd want to go to the barn. He'd want his bridle off so he could get a drink of water at the trough. Then with a nice loose halter on he'd step up over the high sill into the barn and walk down the side aisle until he came to his own stall. And someone like Pa or me would fasten the halter chain in the worn hole and the fork down hay into his manger just for him, and pour wheat or oats into his grain box. Someone would unfasten the buckles and pull off the heavy harness, and carry it over to hang on the wooden pegs on the wall behind his stall. Someone would take a scratchy brush and rub it over his back and sides and legs to take off ticks and burrs and dried mud. And then run a hand along his back and slap him on the rump, and go out and shut the barn door, and he would toss his hay with his nose, and crunch down the best parts first. He would listen to mice rustling overhead in the hayloft, and owls hunting through the night, and finally he would go to sleep on his feet, the way horses do. When they have come home to the barn.

I didn't have any idea what time it was. It had been dark now for a long, long time. I thought about trying to catch up and lead Pet, but she didn't need anybody to lead her now. Head down, one foot after another, she had settled into her going-to-the-barn gait, and nothing would stop her now. Snip was still roped to Pet, and Gypsy to Snip, and Pet's momentum seemed to feed back through Snip into Gypsy, or else Gypsy was just so glad to be near home that she didn't care about her lame leg.

I was walking and stumbling, off to one side of Pet, and sometime I thought about trying to get on one of them and ride, but I knew at the same time that I couldn't have found the strength to climb into the saddle, let alone jump onto a horse's back back. Around me now and then I heard a snort, a sneeze, a cough, and the soft padding of hooves in the snow. That was Prince over there, with Damfool not far behind him. Socks was back there a little, and I thought Molly and Blaze might be the next ones, but all I could see was just white shapes moving against the white. None of the horses paid any attention to me. I guess they thought I was just another horse, heading for the barn.

God—I thought, or maybe I said it out loud—thanks. I don't know why You made horses the way You did, but thanks. And don't bother sending us a tractor. No matter how good it is, a tractor will never follow you home.

My feet were numb now as well as my hands. My socks and boots were wet all the way through, and there were wet patches on the shoulders of my coat where snow had melted. I didn't feel hungry, exactly, but there was this big, empty place inside of me. I tripped over something—a frozen pile of cow manure—and staggered, almost fell.

Then far ahead I began to see little black spots moving against the snow. Well, why not? The horses were big white spots moving through the snow. So spots can move.

One of the spots seemed to be coming toward me. It was moving fast—running—it looked like—

"Trixie!" I whispered.

The little spot turned into a dog shape and then a dog—and Trixie flashed across the snow. Barking and whining she jumped high in the air, licking my face and landing to bounce up again and again.

"Trixie—Trixie—" I fell to my knees and wrapped my arms around her. Her fur was cold and silky and smelled like old bones, and her wet nose made icy little dabs at my face, somehow knowing to be gentle with my eye. "Trixie—"

The other, bigger moving spot came

forward, out of the blurry background of darkness and moving horses. "Wart! Wart! You there? Jesus Christ, boy, where you *been*—?"

Pa opened the corral gate at the barn and waited for the last horse to go through. I tried to count them as I stood there beside him. I thought I only saw eight, but Pa said there were nine. That meant they had all come home except for Ol' Rosie. Hungry and cold and ready for a manger of hay and a can of grain, nine runaway horses had decided that there was a lot to be said for a barn after all.

When the horses were all through the gate, I saw Pa turn once and look back out over the pasture. I knew he was looking for Ol' Rosie, but he didn't say anything. I thought, when he asks me, I'll tell him. But not now.

I stood there leaning against the corral fence while Pa closed the gate. He took the ropes off Pet and Snip and Gypsy, let them all drink at the trough, and then opened the barn door and let them into their stalls, the colt following Pet like a little black shadow.

"Go to the house," said Pa. "I put feed down already. I'll halter them and brush them down. Go to the house, Wart."

But for some reason I couldn't. I stood there by the barn door, just inside, smelling the hay and listening to the halter chains rattle as the horses settled down to hay and grain. To rest, to get warm, to sleep. Maybe to dream about how it had been out there on the cold, snowy ridges, free, no harnesses, no saddles, but no barns, no hay, no grain. For some reason it felt awful good to stand there, listening to Pa talking softly to each of the horses, smelling the hay and the good, clean smell of the barn. And . . . just being there.

When the last horse was tethered in his stall, Pa took his lantern down from the hook on the wall and turned to me. "Come on."

I followed him out into the night. But now, instead of the cold glow of snow there was a splash of yellow light from the lantern that fell over Pa's boots, the ground, and made a bright trail for me to follow. The rhythm of his steps made me think of the rhythm of the horses: pa-*pum*, pa-*pum*, pa-*pum*—

"You should have come home yesterday." Pa's voice came back to me over his shoulder. "You could have killed yourself out there. What happened to your eye?"

"I roped Snip. She drug me."

Pa jerked to a stop and turned to look at me.

"This afternoon," I added. "I didn't catch up with them till this afternoon. Gypsy . . . went lame."

"I seen that." Pa's face was grim. "How come she went lame?"

"Rock . . . turned under her. And . . . she's got some barbwire cuts."

Pa looked at me hard, but I just looked back at him. "I got them back!" I said and I was surprised at how strong my voice was. "I got the horses back, Pa," and I said it quick before he could start to yell at me. "I got them back—all except Ol' Rosie. And you'd have cussed me out if I hadn't brought them home."

Pa stared at me for a long time. He knew I was right. He knew we had to have the horses—otherwise he wouldn't have sent me. At last he raised the lantern and blew it out. As he reached out for the doorknob to open the kitchen door, I said, "Pa."

He looked around.

"Don't call me Wart no more."

The kitchen was warm and bright, with two kerosene lamps burning, one on the table and one on the shelf above the stove. Davy was asleep on the settle, with the same quilt wrapped around him. Had he been there all the time I was gone?

"Get your coat off. And your boots. Set over here by the stove." Pa pulled a kitchen chair close to the stove and then reached up into the cupboard and took out a tin cup. "There's some hot stew. It'll warm you up."

Slowly I dragged myself across to the stove. Seemed farther than all the way I had gone these last two days. "I'm—tired," I whispered. I sat down in the chair. If it hadn't been there, I would have hit the floor. The heat on my face from the stove was queer and foreign somehow, and seemed to sting like nettles rubbed against the skin. I was beginning to feel fuzzy and blurry, and there seemed to be a lot of things hanging around at the back of my mind that I ought to be thinking about, that I ought to be remembering. Important things. But the stove was warm, and I was so cold. . . .

Suddenly something came back to me. The gate. I hadn't been able to get the wire gate closed. "Pa"—I said—"the gate—the wire gate—to the cow pasture. I couldn't get it shut. I tried. I . . . couldn't—"

Pa poured some coffee into a tin mug and now he handed it to me. "Drink this. Then we got to git your boots off. Pull." He leaned over and grabbed one of my boots, then the other. I pulled feebly against his pull, and in a second both boots were off. He peeled my socks off, too, and looked at my feet. "Water," he said. And before I figured out what he meant, he'd put a bucket of water on the floor in front of my chair. "Put your feet in this." The water was lukewarm. My feet began to pulse, then to pound, as the water warmed the patchy white skin. "You could have lost them toes to frostbite."

"Yeah, Pa. But about the gate—"

Pa took my hat off and unbuttoned my coat, peeled my gloves and coat off. Everything was wet in spots and crunchy with ice in other spots. Then he picked up a blanket from somewhere and wrapped it around me. "Forget about the gate," he said. "I'll close it tomorrow." Then suddenly he shouted, "Why the hell didn't you come home yesterday? Christ Jesus, boy, I been out of my mind worryin' about you!"

I looked up at him. Pa? Worrying about *me?* "Why? What for? You told me to bring in the horses—"

"I never meant for you to stay out there all night—two days—you could have got yourself killed—" His hand holding my coat was shaking. It's the only time I ever remember my pa scared.

I looked up at him as I remembered

the snow, the rocks, the cold, the steep ridges, the deep gullies. The cougar. "Pa," I said at last, "can I have some Watkins Salve?" I held out my hand, palm up. The skin around the cuts was lumpy and red. "I . . . cut myself."

I ate four cups of the stew without hardly stopping to breathe. After Pa rubbed some salve on my cuts and wrapped them with strips of cloth, he took the tea kettle off the stove and poured some hot water into the bucket. By the time my stomach was full of stew, my feet felt good. I pulled them out of the water and dried them on a towel he handed me. I still had the feeling there were important things I ought to remember now, now that I was beginning to feel better.

Pa picked up the bucket and carried it over to the door and set it down. He'd throw it to the pigs tomorrow; water's scarce here. "I don't know much to do about your eye now except to wash it," he said. He handed me a rag wrung out of soapy water, and I reached up and pressed it over the bloody patch. It stung and smarted, but I knew it had to be cleaned up, and now. After several changes of rag and water, Pa leaned over and took a good look at it. "Can you . . . see out of it?"

"Yeah. It's just skinned and bloody. Swelled shut. I can still see out of it."

"Tomorrow Ma can look at it—"

In a flash, it all came back. Ma! I knew what it was I had to remember—"Pa"—I stood up even though my knees were shaky—"Ma—how is—is she—all right?"

Pa took the rag from me and put it in the pan of water. He turned to look at me, and now at last I looked at him. His face was thin and tired. He looked as if it had been as hard for him here as it had been for me out there. "Ma's . . . all right," he said at last, and the way he said it, I knew there'd been a time when she wasn't all right.

The fire in the stove ticked softly. I waited.

"Ma . . . she had a real bad time. I thought"—his voice broke, then he stumbled on—"I almost thought—we'd lose her—"

"No!" I made myself breathe once, twice, waiting for him to tell me more. "But—she's all right now? She's okay?"

Pa's shoulders sagged, as if he'd been carrying a heavy weight. "She lost a lot of blood. But it's stopped now. She needs rest. She's going to be in bed for a long time."

One more thing to wait for.

Then Pa's face softened, and he smiled. "Boy," he said, "you got another baby brother."

I climbed the ladder to the loft and I wondered how it would feel to crawl into my bed, feel the quilts, feel warm, feel safe.

Pa was climbing the ladder behind me. I looked back at him, and now I noticed something very strange. I've always thought of Pa as a real big man. He always seemed to be as tall as a pine tree or a mountain. Hard as the rimrocks, strong as the biggest horse. But now all at once I saw that he isn't all that tall. He is taller than me—but not all that much. Maybe he isn't that hard, either, or that strong. . . .

I pulled my jeans off and sat down on the bunk, and then lay back, pulling the quilts up to my chin.

Pa came to the side of the bed and stood there, looking down at me. "I—I was scared to death," he said. "I didn't know if I'd sent you out . . . to kill yourself."

I looked up at him. "We had to have the horses back. And I'm all right, Pa. I'll be okay." It felt funny to be telling Pa, "I'll be okay." But I could see he needed that. And as I could see him smaller now, I knew all at once that he was seeing me bigger. It was a funny feeling.

"Tomorrow," I said, "I want to see the baby."

"Yeah. Tomorrow. He's got red hair, like Ma."

"That's nice."

"Go to sleep."

"Yeah . . ."

"Good night . . . John." He turned and climbed down the ladder.

In the darkness I looked up to where

the rafters were, the roof, and it was like I could look beyond that to the clouds, the dark night sky. God was up there, Ma always says. I used to want to ask her how she knew that. It may be that she just figured it out. But if she didn't really figure it out, maybe she just kept on walking toward it till she understood it, like I kept on walking after the horses—because there is no other way to get where you have to go.

And as I lay there feeling the warmth and comfort of the bed and the house strong and safe around me like that fort in the wilderness that I had thought about—was it only yesterday morning?—I began to think on toward tomorrow. Tomorrow I would see the new baby, and tease Davy about not being the baby of the family anymore. And Davy and I could make a snowman. He'd like that. In the evening after Davy was asleep, I'd work on whittling out his toy boat. Or maybe . . . maybe I'd try to find a picture of a tractor, and whittle out one of those for him. Of course, he wouldn't know what a tractor was, but maybe I could explain it a little.

Someday . . . we would all know about tractors. But not now. Not for a while longer.
For now it would be horses and harnesses
and runaways, and long, hard rides. . . .

And in the morning I'd give Pa a hand
with the chores and tell Pa and Ma about
the horses and making camp last night,
and how I'd finally caught first Pet and
then Snip. I would tell them about the
cougar. And how Ol' Rosie had killed the
cougar, and how she'd paid her devil back
and gotten rid of him, and how she had to
go free now forever. I had a feeling that it
was something I had to remember, too—
because someday I might have a devil of
my own to fight against. I had to be sure to
think of the right way to say it all.

But I would do all that tomorrow. . . .